# HOUSE OF DEATH

## *Dr Hamlet Mottrell Series*
## *Book Three*

## Michael Fowler

SAPERE
BOOKS

# HOUSE OF DEATH

Published by Sapere Books.

24 Trafalgar Road, Ilkley, LS29 8HH

**saperebooks.com**

ISBN: 978-1-80055-933-2

# ONE

## CORPSE BRIDES KILLER IN COURT
### Matt Ross, Crime Correspondent

*A man held on suspicion of the abduction and murder of five women will appear in court tomorrow as police seek to question him further.*

*This paper was the first to break the news of the gruesome discovery made inside an abandoned World War II bunker on the outskirts of Sheffield twelve days ago, and we have now learned that the man being questioned is a serving police officer with the South Yorkshire Police.*

*We can reveal that one of the victims is 24-year-old Elise Farmer, a former student at the University of Sheffield who disappeared five years ago whilst walking her dog on a popular tourist trail near Grassington in North Yorkshire. Her disappearance sparked a county-wide search before the investigation was scaled back.*

*We have contacted the Chief Constable for comment regarding the arrest of one of his officers, but so far the Force has remained tight-lipped. The Police and Crime Commissioner has said that he is unable to comment on an ongoing investigation, or on the identity of the man they have in custody, but he wants to reassure the public that they are safe on the streets of South Yorkshire, and that extra patrols, especially in the evenings, have been put in place.*

*The case has, however, raised questions as to whether the officer in custody could be responsible for other unsolved missing persons cases. As the Independent Office for Police Conduct launch their own investigation, this newspaper is calling for a public inquiry to determine exactly what South Yorkshire Police knew about the officer's background and whether there has been any cover-up.*

With a heavy sigh Dr Hamlet Mottrell closed down his computer. It had been the third time he had read the article, and with each reread, he had felt every sentence corrode his wellbeing further. It had been a long week and he was glad it was Friday. He reached for his mobile to ring his friend and supervisor, Detective Sergeant Alix Rainbow. She answered almost immediately. He said sharply, 'Have you seen the *Sheffield Telegraph*?'

'Just read it, Hamlet,' Alix answered. 'I can't say I didn't see it coming after all the publicity from Nate's arrest, but this is not going to help the pressure we're already under.'

Detective Constable Nathaniel Fox, known as Nate, had fooled them all. The young detective had managed to deceive his colleagues by hiding in plain sight whilst investigating the case of the so-called 'Wedding Killer', a serial killer responsible for the abduction and murder of five young women whose bodies had been discovered embalmed and wearing wedding dresses. Now they knew he had been responsible all along for the brutal deaths, yet the shock had yet to fade.

'Are we interviewing him today?'

'I've just spoken with the boss and she tells me that Nate's not going before the magistrates until this afternoon, and by the time everything is sorted it's going to be well into the day. She wants us to put together an interview strategy for tomorrow and check on how forensics are getting on with searching his home.'

'Have they found anything else beside the discs?' Several DVDs had been recovered from a secret room in the cellar of Nate's house, which featured footage of a masked person murdering each of the victims — evidence that pointed the finger at Nate.

'Not so far.'

'Anything on his computer?'

'The techies are still working on it. He's not cooperating. Refusing to tell them his password. Same with his phone and tablet. He's not said anything to anyone since we showed him the discs we found hidden at his home. Complete silence.'

Hamlet nodded. 'That's not uncommon among serial killers. Whilst some are proud to explain why they did what they did, the majority fail to take responsibility for their actions even when faced with damning evidence. Nate has even more to lose, being a cop. From what I know about him, he's probably enjoying pitting his wits against us. And on that note, have you seen that bit in the paper about the possibility of him being responsible for other missing persons? Has someone said something? Do you think someone on the team has talked?'

'No. The team is solid. The press are just second-guessing. They know it's something we'll be looking at.'

'Okay. I'll see you on Monday.'

'You will.' She paused. 'You know something, former forensic psychologist Dr Hamlet Mottrell, you're shaping up into a good detective. I know I can trust you with putting the interview strategy together. It will be right up your street. Interviewing a serial killer is second-nature for you.'

# TWO

Outside the chapel, Alix was among the hundred-strong crowd who had come to Elise Farmer's celebration of life service. She was watching the three-car funeral cortège approach, bowing her head in reverence as it slowly passed. As the cars drew to a stop beneath the entrance canopy, a lump jerked in her throat. She had been dreading this day ever since they had discovered Elise's body two weeks previously, because, although she was there in her professional capacity, saying goodbye to the first of Nate's victims, she was also there as Elise's friend.

There was a choreographed opening of car doors, and Alix watched Elise's parents and her husband ease themselves out from the second black limo and come together into a huddle, each of them wiping away tears and setting their sorrowful gaze upon Elise's coffin being respectfully handled out of the lead funeral car by the pall bearers. Alix didn't recognise anyone climbing out of the third limo and wondered if they were family members or former work colleagues. She already knew that Elise's husband, Daniel, had moved on with his life; he had a new partner and nine months ago their daughter had been born. Alix had felt so sad when she'd heard that news from Elise's mother. She knew that Elise had been trying for a baby with Daniel before her disappearance five years ago. She would have made a great mother. Nate Fox had taken that away from her when he took her life. *The bastard.*

As the group shuffled towards the doors of the chapel, Alix held back. Although she knew Elise's family well, she was still there in an official capacity and had a job to do. Once inside the chapel, she slipped into the back pew where she could observe the congregation. She especially wanted to keep her eyes on the journalists she had spotted. If any of them stepped out of line, she wouldn't hesitate to drag them outside and give them an ear-bashing; Alix had spoken daily with Elise's mum since they had found her daughter's body, professionally and as a friend, and she had complained about the press banging on their front door for a story. This had worsened following the revelation that Elise's killer was none other than one of the detectives involved in the investigation into her disappearance and murder. Listening to Elise's mum's sobs, she had wanted to beat the living daylights out of Nate Fox for his treacherous acts, and the members of the media who were repeatedly haranguing Elise's family.

Her thoughts were suddenly interrupted by music striking up; Beethoven's 'Für Elise'. It had been one of the early pieces of music Alix had learned to play during her piano lessons as a child back home with her parents. When she had first played this on a clapped-out pub piano during one of their many Friday night bar crawls and told her the title, Elise had been so taken aback that she had made her play it three times more until a drunken customer had shouted at them to 'stop playing that crap' and marched across to slam down the piano lid. Elise had thrown her lager over him and they'd had to make a run for it.

Alix had played the piece many times since, thinking of Elise. *Elise must have told her parents about the tune.* She could feel herself starting to well up and switched into work mode, drifting her gaze around the chapel to see who she could recognise.

Sara, Jasmine and Claire, friends from her time at university with Elise, were seated together four rows in front. Claire was already dabbing her eyes with a tissue. Beyond them, Alix's eyes rested upon the celebrant at the front lectern. Dressed in a blue suit with a matching mustard-coloured tie and handkerchief, he looked more like a city financier than a celebrant, and as she took in his relaxed air Alix realised she knew him. Within seconds it came to her. Alan Leonard. He had delivered the service for her former colleague Sam Reese, who had been stabbed outside a convenience store and who'd died in her arms.

She had been a probationer at the time. Sam had been her tutor and working partner. He'd also been her lover, despite being married. It had been the worst day of her police career. She had cried all the way through Sam's service, despite Alan delivering one of the funniest and most moving send-offs she had heard. He had later turned up at the wake in the pub, and she and some of her colleagues had chatted with him. He had regaled them with stories from some of his memorial services with such wicked wit that he had taken away the sombreness of that day. Knowing Elise's zest for life and sense of humour, Alix could see why her parents had chosen Alan to pay their final tributes.

'There are no words adequate, no words that can soften the blow when we are faced with the shock of an unexpected death. But when that death is a tragic one, there does not seem to be any point in searching for meaning or a sense of comfort...'

The opening made Alix sit up, breaking her reflections and pulling her back into the moment.

'Everyone has been shocked and saddened by what happened to Elise, but we are here today to celebrate her life and not her death.'

This raised another lump in Alix's throat, and she had to gulp back a sob. When Alan mentioned that her family wanted this to be an occasion on which to share memories of the times spent with Elise, her mind instantly flashed back to the night she'd collapsed in her room at the university halls ten years ago. It had happened a year to the day following her rape. Until then, she had managed to put on a front at lectures and even whilst out socially, even though mentally, she was mess. Nights had been her worst moments, when her mind repeatedly replayed the attack in terrifying flashbacks.

In her nightmares the man in the ski mask was always there, standing over her with a knife. Her screaming had regularly awakened Elise, who had occupied the room next door, and she had repeatedly rushed to her aid, spending many a sleepless night sitting with her, coaxing her to talk about her ordeal. Following her breakdown, Alix had blurted out that she was contemplating suicide and that was when Elise had introduced her to the Samaritans, where she had been working as a volunteer. The help from her Samaritan counsellor had stopped her from taking her life, even though it was at the forefront of her thoughts for many months.

Within six months she was again coping with everything university life threw at her. She continued with her course, got a 2.1 in social work studies, but then decided to join the police in the hope of tracking down her attacker.

Elise had been her saviour. For a split second the image of Elise garbed in that second-hand wedding dress, her embalmed corpse hideously made-up like a doll, flashed before her eyes. She now knew that Elise had been repeatedly raped in the bunker where they had found her, and from her own experience Alix understood what she must have gone through. What she couldn't and didn't want to think about was what had gone through her friend's mind when she had realised she was going to die. That must have been horrific. She hoped Nate would get his just deserts in prison.

*Rot in hell, you bastard.*

The celebrant's voice brought her back to the present. 'The time has come when we say a final farewell to Elise. We thank her for being a wonderful wife, daughter, and friend. The world has been a richer place for having her in it.'

Alix took a deep breath, letting it out slowly, her eyes focused on the deep red drapes that were slowly closing, cutting off the view of Elise's coffin.

The celebrant bowed his head and the congregation followed suit.

'Elise, we send you on to the next part of your journey with our love and care. Even though you are precious to us, we let you go. Carrying with you all the beauty of life which we have shared with you, Elise, we release you…'

Alix heard no more of the celebrant's farewell. Tears rolled down her cheeks, stinging the corners of her mouth.

Alix stayed in her pew as the congregation slowly drifted out of the chapel. She was in no mood to exchange sorrow-laden chit-chat with anyone. All she wanted was to go home and lie down. Watching the last person leave, she counted to ten before rising and heading for the exit, but as she reached the door she saw Elise's mother waiting for her.

Mrs Lewis instantly made a beeline for her, holding out her hands in greeting. 'I was hoping I hadn't missed you, Alix,' she said, taking hold of one of Alix's hands and giving it a gentle squeeze. 'I saw you at the back and wanted to thank you personally for coming.' Her mouth broke into a smile, but it looked strained.

Alix could feel herself welling up again. 'It was a lovely service,' she answered, the words catching in her throat.

'It was, wasn't it? Are you coming back for a drink and bite to eat?'

'I'd love to, Mrs Lewis, but I'm expected back at work.' It was a lie. A blinding headache had come on and she needed peace and quiet. She would text her boss when she got home and take the rest of the day off. She knew Detective Inspector Lauren Simmerson would understand, and Hamlet was more than capable of undertaking the task she had left him with.

Mrs Lewis gave her hand another squeeze. 'I understand, Alix. Please keep in touch.'

'Sure, Mrs Lewis, I'll let you know what's happening.'

'No, I don't mean work, Alix. Call in and have a cuppa when you're passing or at a loose end. You're always welcome. It's been nice catching up with you this past week, even given the circumstances.'

'I will, I promise. I'll pop over to see you in a couple of days.'

'I'll hold you to that, Alix. Thank you again for all you've done.'

Alix's drive home was nerve-jangling. Her vision had narrowed, with dots jumping around the back of her eyes, as her headache worsened. At one stage she thought she would throw up and powered down all the windows, sucking in gulps of cool air to hold back the sickness.

As she pulled up outside her Victorian town house, she was grateful to find there was space to park; generally, by the time she got home, all available parking spaces had been taken and she had to search one out in the nearby side streets. Sometimes it could be a two- or three-hundred-metre trudge home — a pain when she'd had a gruelling day and felt drained. At least she wouldn't have to suffer that today.

Dragging out her bag and locking the car, she walked up to the front door, unlocked its five-lever lock, waited for the alarm to start beeping, and then stepped into the hall, quickly slamming the door behind her, securing the deadbolt and putting on the chain. The chain was a recent addition to her home-security following her abduction two weeks ago.

Thankfully, unlike the other victims of Nate Fox, she had been found before she had come to any harm. She'd lain, tied up, in a garage pit for three days, where it had gone through her mind that she was going to suffer the same fate as Elise and the other victims. The euphoria that had swept through her when police had found her would stay with her for a long time.

Despite being rescued, the experience had triggered the return of her panic attacks. However, this time she could recognise the symptoms the moment they started and had been able to deal with them — even when interviewing Nate, the man whom she now suspected of raping her all those years ago.

Since his arrest she had done a lot of soul-searching, wondering how on earth she had missed the signs. Even with all her training and previous experience of interviewing rapists, she hadn't been able to detect that her closest colleague, the man sitting across from her, was a murderer and perhaps her rapist. Without warning her thoughts spiralled back to that night at her parent's vicarage, when she and her parents had been confronted by a masked knife-wielding man they thought was a burglar. What he did to her changed her life. Her faith, once so strong, had taken a massive knock and it had strained her relationship with her parents — especially with her dad, whom she blamed for not protecting her. Now her dad was ill with bowel cancer, and yet she still used any excuse to avoid going to see them because she couldn't sleep there anymore, and she knew how much that hurt them. It had destroyed all their lives.

*Fucking Nate Fox!* She had made a solemn promise to Elise's parents that she would bring their daughter's killer to justice, and a promise to herself for what he'd done to her. And that was exactly what she was going to do. No one was going to stop her from making him suffer.

# THREE

Hamlet gave up trying to sleep well before dawn, leaving for work early, his mind going over the questions he'd planned for his and Alix's interview with Nate later that morning.

As he turned into the narrow slip-road that led to the car park for the Major Investigation Team building, he found himself facing a barricade of journalists and TV reporters. He slapped down the visor and tucked his chin into his chest as he eased his Range Rover through the scrum, accelerating away to find a parking spot that was as far away from the media circus as possible. The last thing he needed was his face pasted all over the telly. Again. The publicity haunting the Homicide and Major Enquiry Team was bad enough, but the revelation that the one-time prime suspect in the spree-murder of his own family was now a rookie detective in the same squad as a suspected serial killer would be disastrous.

Fortunately, and with Alix's help, Hamlet had been able to prove his innocence and catch the real killer. The person responsible for the brutal murder of his wife Helen and their unborn child, as well as his adoptive parents, was a former patient at the psychiatric unit where Hamlet had worked.

Hitching up the collar of his jacket, Hamlet snatched his briefcase from the back seat and quick-marched to the glass entrance, keeping his head low until he reached the reception area, where he headed straight for the lift. Getting out at the first floor he found the landing eerily silent, reminding him just how early it was. Generally, the team drifted in at around a quarter to eight. This would allow him plenty of time to make a cup of tea and go through the interview strategy he had compiled, before everyone piled in and fractured his concentration.

Entering the office, he was surprised to see Alix already at her desk, taking a bite out of a piece of toast. She looked up as he strode over. 'This is a surprise. Thought I'd be the first in,' he said, putting down his briefcase.

'Couldn't sleep,' she mumbled, putting down the slice of toast, wiping her hands on some tissue and taking a sip of water from a bottle.

Hamlet had already learned that Alix always put on a resolute front at work, but this morning was different. She looked drained. He said, 'How did Elise's funeral go?'

'So, so, as far as funerals go. I didn't go to the wake. Couldn't face it.'

'Want to talk about it?'

'Not just now, Hamlet, thanks. Maybe later.' She picked up her toast again.

'I'm just going to make myself a cup of tea. Want one?'

'Got this, thanks.' She lifted up her bottle of water. 'Anyway, what're you doing in so early?'

'Couldn't sleep either. All the stuff to do with Nate.' He slipped off his jacket and wound it around the back of his seat. 'I'll make myself a drink, and then I'll need you to read through what I've put in the strategy to see if I've got all the exhibits in order.'

As he set off across the room to put the kettle on, Alix called to him. 'Given your previous work as a forensic psychologist, what are your thoughts on the possibility Nate may be responsible for more murders?'

'I've given that a lot of thought. I've re-looked at everything relating to the five women he abducted and killed, particularly the method he used. What stands out is the lack of witnesses to any of the abductions. Each of our victims simply vanished. That tells me he is extremely methodical. We know from the timeline that Elise was his first victim. She went missing five years ago. And we know from people we've spoken to since Nate's arrest that he actually knew Elise six years before she was abducted, from their time together at university. I've already shared with you that it is my belief that he began stalking Elise at that time. I suspect he followed her down to your parent's vicarage when she visited you during the summer, and that due to circumstances it was you he attacked instead of her. If that is the case, then I have to question what he's been up to in the years between attacking you and abducting Elise. Six years is a long time.' He paused, before adding, 'I think there may be more victims out there. Dead or alive.'

Alix was about to respond when DI Lauren Simmerson appeared in the doorway.

'I thought I heard voices,' she said. 'I need to talk with the pair of you. Can you come down?' With that, Lauren turned on her heel and disappeared.

Hamlet and Alix looked at one another with raised eyebrows.

'Wonder what's up,' Alix said, pushing herself up from her desk.

Lauren's office was a short distance along the corridor, opaque floor-to-ceiling glass hiding its interior. The DI had left the door open and Hamlet saw that Detective Chief Inspector Karl Henry Jackson was already seated with Lauren at her small conference table.

Lauren motioned them in with her hand and signalled them to be seated.

Hamlet sensed nothing good about this sudden meeting, especially with the DCI being there. As he sat down, his stomach began to churn.

'What's the matter, boss?' Alix asked, sitting down.

Lauren rested her elbows on the desk, pressing the tips of her fingers together. Her face looked solemn. 'We need to have a word with the pair of you.'

Hamlet straightened the creases in his trousers as he sat, flicking his gaze between the DI and DCI. Their solemn faces spoke volumes. He had a bad feeling about this.

'Alix and Hamlet,' Jackson opened, clearing his throat, 'there's no easy way to say this, but I'm afraid I am not the bringer of good news this morning.'

'Is this about Nate?' Alix asked.

Jackson nodded, the top of his shaved head shiny under the fluorescent ceiling lights. 'Lauren and I have just come back from a meeting with the Chief. As you know, the force has not had good publicity this week. The public outrage has been relentless, especially regarding the allegations that we covered up Nate's crimes…'

'That's ridiculous, boss,' interjected Alix. 'If it hadn't been for Hamlet, the wrong person would have been accused.'

Jackson held up a hand. 'Believe me, Alix, I'm on your side. I know about all the hard work that went into this investigation, and how diligent you have been, but I need to show you something that the Chief received yesterday. It might change things somewhat.' Jackson turned over a clear plastic evidence bag he had been covering with his hand and slid it into the middle of the table. Inside was an A4-sized sheet of paper, upon which was typed lettering.

In silence, Hamlet and Alix read it.

*Hi Chief Pig, don't think for one minute you've caught me. Those women's bodies you've found are down to me and not that little pig of yours languishing in his pen. You give me credit for them and I might just confess to the others.*

*I'll be in touch soon.*

Alix's head shot up. 'That's bollocks,' she blurted. 'It's from some crank. You know we get stuff like this all the time. Nate's responsible for these killings.'

'That's as may be, Alix, but you and I both know we can't ignore this. And certainly, the Chief's got to take this seriously because of all the publicity surrounding the murders. This note was left under the wipers of a police car parked up near Sheffield Courts yesterday afternoon while Nate Fox was facing the magistrates. Unfortunately, that spot is not covered by CCTV, so we have no idea who is responsible. One thing is for certain: it wasn't Nate.

'We've also learned this morning that an identical letter has been sent to several daily papers, who are now clamouring for comment and questioning whether we've got the right person. It will make the headline news this lunchtime. As a result, the Police and Crime Commissioner received a call from a senior minister from the Home Secretary's office. She's decided to send in another force to carry out an urgent review of the investigation.

'And if that's not enough, Nate's solicitor is alleging that his client has been fitted up. We've had a journalist contact us from the BBC. They are planning on running a *Panorama* special and they've already interviewed Nate's solicitor. He claims that Nate is the victim of a miscarriage of justice because he gave Hamlet a hard time when he investigated him for the murders of his family. This is a vendetta by Hamlet in return.

'He is also blaming Lauren for allowing Hamlet to be a member of the team, given the circumstances of the crimes he was investigated for. In addition, he's hinting that your relationship with Hamlet, Alix, is more than just a working one, and that it's interfering with your professional judgement. He's citing all these things in an application for Nate to be released from custody.'

'That's absolute bullshit. What about the evidence we've got against him? The discs we found at his house?' exclaimed Alix.

Hamlet remained silent. He realised that as a rookie detective, he would have to bite his tongue for the moment. Anyway, Alix was doing a pretty good job fighting their corner.

Jackson held up his hand again. 'I get what you're saying, Alix, but we can't ignore this note and the letters to the newspapers. Nate's solicitor claims that the DVDs you found at his home, which show the victims being killed, have, first of all, been planted, and second, the masked person in them is not his client. We've had the discs forensically tested and can confirm that they are copies. We've not found any originals during our search. And as you know, although we've seized Nate's computer, tablet and phone, we've not been able to get into them yet, so there is nothing by way of evidence to counter-challenge what is being alleged. As we speak a team is being pulled together to scrutinise the evidence, as well as every decision that's been made and every action we've carried out relating to this case so far.'

'This is crazy. Is there nothing you can do? This is just like the Yorkshire Ripper inquiry with that hoax tape. It diverted the entire investigation away from Peter Sutcliffe. That's what's happening here with that letter.' Alix stabbed a finger at the evidence wallet in the centre of the table.

'We are bearing that in mind, but we can't ignore it.'

'And Nate's solicitor is prejudicing our investigation,' huffed Alix. 'Can't you do anything about that?'

Jackson shook his head. 'His actions are unorthodox, but he's not doing anything illegal. I've tried to fight our corner, but it's been taken out of my hands. I've been instructed that everything you've got relating to the investigation is to be handed over with immediate effect.'

'What about all the statements we've taken and the outstanding enquiries? What about the possibility there may be more victims? There's still such a lot to do.'

Jackson shrugged his shoulders. 'That's now down to whoever is coming in to do the review. And the same team will be looking at whether this note is from some crank or not. All I can advise is to put what you've got into a semblance of order and hand it over. We know this is a paper exercise because of the Home Secretary's interference, but it has to be done. If there is the remotest chance of casting doubt over the case against his client, then Nate's lawyer will grasp it. The Chief wants all the boxes ticking, given that the Home Secretary and Parliament is scrutinising this case.'

'So, we just stand there twiddling our thumbs while they shred our case?' Alix demanded, clearly irritated.

DCI Jackson glanced at Lauren before replying. 'Well, I'm afraid there's some more bad news, Alix. You are off the case until further notice. Due to the allegations of corruption by Nate's solicitor, I have been instructed by the Chief to remove the pair of you from this investigation…'

'What?' Alix said, her voice rising.

'I'm afraid it doesn't stop there. My orders are that you are to work remotely for the time being...'

'Work remotely?'

Jackson nodded. 'In effect, you are both put on gardening leave until this is sorted out. You are to gather your personal things from the office and leave with immediate effect.'

# FOUR

'Unbelievable. Un-fucking-believable,' Alix fumed.

Hamlet sipped the head off his beer with a loud sucking noise. He and Alix were seated at one of the picnic tables in the courtyard of the Boat Inn, a pub that overlooked the canal basin at Sprotbrough, a quarter of a mile from the woodland where he lived in his off-the-grid cabin. They had driven there for a much-needed drink after being escorted out of the MIT building as if they were villains.

'I know Nate and I never really hit it off, but I never set out to target him as a killer. I can't believe he's accusing me of planting those DVDs,' he said now.

'Because you found him out, that's why. He thought he'd got away with it. He'd fixed someone else to take the fall and you stopped him in his tracks. It's his last throw of the dice — that's why he's made the allegations.' Alix took a long swallow of her lager. 'Personally, I feel humiliated. I would have expected more support from the bosses. They know we haven't stitched him up. That note's a distraction. Nothing more.'

'I'm annoyed too, Alix, but I can see there was very little else the DCI could do. The Chief Constable's hands are tied because of the adverse publicity, and now this note, which claims the real killer is still out there. Nate's solicitor has just jumped on the bandwagon, adding more pressure on the force. Think about it. The case has made international headlines, and now the Home Secretary is involved. The Chief had to do something in view of all the allegations. I'm sure the force reviewing our investigation will see that everything has been done by the book and reinstate us.'

Alix scowled. 'And how long will that take? Six months? And in the meantime Nate's solicitor could get him released on bail until the investigation concludes. I couldn't bear for that to happen, knowing what he did to Elise and the others.'

'Surely they wouldn't allow that? He's being questioned over five murders.'

'Innocent until proven guilty,' Alix replied, sounding exasperated. 'There's always some bleeding-heart judge willing to be persuaded. Especially if Nate gets the right barrister. They all piss in the same pot.'

'Like cops, you mean,' Hamlet answered, a mischievous smile playing on his lips.

Alix burst out laughing. 'Okay, smart-ass. But don't forget you're one of us now.'

'Too young in the job to be corrupted, though, aren't I? If I'm interviewed, I'll just say you were the one in charge. I followed your instructions,' he replied, returning a dead-pan look.

'You can talk. It's *you* he's blaming. It was *you* who found the evidence that pointed the finger at him.'

Hamlet took another drink. 'Do you think I got it wrong? You heard what the gaffer said — the discs I found showing Elise and the others being murdered are copies. And so far, there's no forensic evidence linking him to the bodies. Could those DVDs have been planted in Nate's house by the real killer? To throw us off the track?'

'If that's the case, why leave a note declaring they're the killer?'

'Baiting us?'

Alix shook her head. 'I'm not buying that. Both my experience and gut tell me that letter is from some crank, and as for the lack of evidence, that's only because Nate was so smart when the call came in about the bodies being found. He was one of the first at the scene, so he can argue that any evidence linking him was from his attendance.' Pausing, she added, 'I'm one hundred per cent sure you made the right call, Hamlet, but it's so frustrating not being able to prove it. The team they'll be bringing in to review it will be doing just that. They won't be working on the investigation. That'll be back to us when they realise we haven't done anything wrong and reinstate us, and God only knows when that will be. And in the meantime Nate's solicitor might just be able to persuade a judge to let him out on bail.'

'Is there nothing we can do? Before we were sent packing this morning we were going to check up on Nate's background, see what he was up to before he joined the police. See if he's linked to any other missing persons or unsolved murders. Can't we do that? It's not as though we'll be interfering with the work the review team will be doing. And it'll be one less job we'll need to do once the review is complete.'

'Great idea, but we don't have access to any of the police systems.'

'We've got the internet.'

'True. But that might not be enough. We could really do with our case notes to cross-reference what we find. And we don't have those, do we?'

Hamlet looked smug. 'Not the originals, no. But you may recall I copied everything so I could go through the investigation at home? I've even got copies of the photographs.'

Flashing a grin, Alix responded, 'Words fail me, Hamlet. Some of us go home after work and switch on the news or some shit police drama that we shout at for getting it all wrong, but not you. You take home copies of the investigation so you can work on them.'

'Is that your way of saying that I'm an absolute genius?'

'I wouldn't go that far, but you have just been awarded a gold star.' Alix downed the remainder of her lager. 'Well, come on then, what are you waiting for? Sup up and get your arse in gear. You and I have got a killer to nail.'

Closing and padlocking his five-bar gate, Hamlet jumped back into his Range Rover and led the way along the uneven woodland path, slowly turning into the clearing and pulling up in front of his cabin. Alix followed in her black Audi, parking behind him.

Skipping up the steps onto the veranda, Hamlet pulled open the French doors, eager to begin work. The moment they were open, his terrier, Lucky, jumped up at his legs, tail wagging. Hamlet reached down and stroked the little dog's head. 'Hello, boy, brought your pal here to see you,' he said, stepping into his cabin.

As if understanding, Lucky peeled off to his armchair, quickly snatching up his teddy before returning to Alix, offering it up. She made a grab for it, but the dog whipped it away from her grasp and backed away fast, tail still wagging.

'That's not very friendly,' Alix chuckled, making another attempt at grabbing the toy. This time Lucky dodged sideways and scampered back to his chair. 'You're too quick for me, little fellow,' she said, following him back to the armchair and ruffling his fur.

Hamlet slipped the knot from his tie, pulled it through his collar and laid it on the table. Releasing the top button of his shirt, he made his way to the kitchen. 'I'll make us a hot drink and you can make a start if you want. Everything is still in my study.'

The study had been constructed by a craftsman joiner for his grandfather, who'd had the cabin built. It was grand in the extreme with two wood-panelled walls and two floor-to-ceiling bookcases, crammed with an eclectic mix of titles on medicine, art, adventure fiction and thrillers. Light poured through a pair of doors that opened out into the woods, and facing them was a huge wooden desk with a leather inlay.

Hamlet had told Alix that his grandfather had used the place as his retreat to come and paint and read, and that as a young boy he'd come here to stay with him, especially during school holidays. As she gazed around the magnificent office room, her eyes fixed upon the pinboard on the panelled wall to her left. It was almost as big as the incident board at work, and every inch of space was filled with photographs and notes with Hamlet's hard-to-read handwriting — typical doctor's scrawl — captioning each of the photos. The display replicated the 'Wedding Killer' investigation, with pictures of the five victims, their details and timeline beneath their photos. At the centre of the montage was a shot of the victims' embalmed corpses dressed in bridal gowns in the makeshift chapel of the World War Two bunker.

*Hamlet's missed nothing out*, she thought, spotting Nate Fox's photograph pinned in the bottom right-hand corner, the word SUSPECT written beneath.

'What do you want to focus on?'

Hamlet's voice made her jump. 'Jesus, don't sneak up on me like that,' she said, spinning around, clasping the middle of her chest.

He gave a short laugh and strolled across to his desk, setting their drinks down.

Alix couldn't help but notice the many documents piled up on the desk. Alongside the computer and keyboard, the entire space was covered. 'Is that the entire inquiry?' she asked, pointing at the paperwork.

'Well, except for the HOLMES information, yes.'

She broke into a smile. 'You really must get out more, you know, Hamlet.'

He smiled back. 'You can mock, but if it wasn't for me doing this, you'd be stuck twiddling your thumbs at home right now.'

'You've got me there.' She picked up her coffee, blew on it, and took a sip while eyeing the papers covering the desk.

'Where do you want to start, then?' Hamlet asked.

'I'd really like to do some research into Nate's background, as we had planned before this morning went to shit.'

'How far back do you want to go?'

'Certainly back to when he was a teenager, before he joined the job.' Pausing, she took another sip of coffee and turned her gaze to Hamlet's pinboard. 'Now that I think about it, I really know very little about him.'

'What do you mean?'

'Well, for instance, I first got to know him when we were in uniform, chatting about what we were going to do at the weekend. I'd usually tell him I was catching up with my friends from uni, and his usual response was, "I'm just going to chill out, watch TV." Other times he would say he "needed to catch up with his washing and sorting the house." I can remember thinking on more than one occasion, *What a boring twat.*'

'Nothing wrong with that. He lived alone. That's what I do.'

'Now you do, Hamlet. But before what happened to your family, I know you and Helen went out together — the cinema, a restaurant. I can't remember Nate ever mentioning going out with his mates, or seeing his parents. And I certainly can't recall him ever mentioning a girlfriend, because I distinctly remember wondering if he might be gay.'

'So, nothing at all about socialising with friends or family?'

'Not that I can recall. I remember one brief conversation with him, when I was talking about my parents. I asked about his and he replied, "Nothing to say about them. They're both dead." That was it. No explanation as to what happened to them. Nothing. In fact, he changed the subject, which made me think that either something bad had happened to them, or that they weren't close and he didn't want to talk about it, so I never probed further. And as for socialising, the only time he went for a drink was straight after work with the team.' Alix's eyes strayed to the ceiling. 'Even when we were partners in CID, he was a closed book as far as his personal life was concerned. I'd never even been to his house before we got the warrant to search it.'

Hamlet was thoughtful, then he asked, 'Do you know where he's from? Where he lived before he got his house at Darnall? Weren't you at university together?'

'We were, but he was a year ahead of me. I certainly don't recall seeing him at Rag week, although that's not surprising because everyone wore fancy dress. Looking back on it now, when we did talk about our uni days, it was usually me who did the talking — mostly about the parties I went to. He told me that he shared digs with a few guys and that they'd occasionally go into town at the weekend, but not to parties. That was the only time he mentioned any type of socialising whatsoever.

'Do you know, Hamlet, this conversation has reinforced how little I know Nate. We were in uniform together and then partners in MIT for two years. I know more about your background than his.'

'Not such a great detective then, after all?' Hamlet joked.

'Funny. But I tell you what — I'm going to make it my business to find out everything I can about him. My first port of call is Personnel. I know one of the women there. I'm sure today's events won't yet have been broadcast. I'll give her a call and ask her to email me Nate's file. Then we can take it from there.'

# FIVE

Nathaniel Fox's personnel file pinged across to Alix's phone while she was outside eating a sandwich on the veranda. She forwarded it to Hamlet's email address, finished her lunch, and then went back indoors to the study, where Hamlet printed off two copies, handing one over to Alix.

Alix was the first to finish reading. Pushing back her chair, she let out a frustrated 'harrumph,' and patted together the loose sheets of paper into a semblance of neatness.

Hamlet still had a couple of pages to read through, but he had the same feeling of frustration. He said, 'There's nothing helpful in this at all. I thought police officers went through serious vetting before they got into the force. I know I did before I was accepted.'

'They do, or at least they should do. Sure, Nate's file lists all the training he's undergone and the courses he's been on, but it doesn't tell us much about his background, other than that he was born and schooled in Devon, that his parents, Joe and Kate Fox, both died fourteen years ago, and that he came to Sheffield to study law at the university when he was eighteen, got a two-one, and then joined the police when he was twenty-one. He has two rental addresses listed, one when he was a student, and one when he joined the police. He bought his house in Darnall five years ago.'

'Not a lot of help,' interjected Hamlet.

'Bugger all, if you ask me.' Alix shook her head. 'He's certainly been very secretive.'

'Deliberately so. And not surprising.'

'I can't believe he was stalking my friend Elise throughout uni, and yet I can't ever recall seeing him hanging around her. Not once.'

Hamlet gave a shrug. 'Don't beat yourself up. You were a teenager. Back then, your only thoughts would have been about getting your work in on time and partying.' He added with a smirk, 'Mostly partying.' Continuing, he said, 'The last thing you would have imagined was that a serial murderer was following you and your friends about.'

'No, of course not, but I wish I had. It might have prevented the attack on me. Elise would still be alive. And I wouldn't be the hot mess that I am today.'

'You're not to blame for any of Nate's crimes, Alix.' Hamlet tapped the pages in front of him. 'People with psychopathic personality disorder share certain traits, including predatory behaviour and a lack of remorse or guilt. His file here reinforces the fact that he's been deliberately secretive so as not to draw attention to himself. It's our job now to prove to others that we were right all along and bring Nate to justice.'

'That's all well and good, Hamlet, but *how* are we going to prove it? We can't go in to work and we can't use any of the police computer systems.'

'That doesn't mean we can't do anything. This is my first official case. I have a personal investment in resolving it. Nate has played cat-and-mouse with me for a while, but I found the evidence that pointed to him and now I want to make it stick. For now, he and his solicitor have prevented us from moving forward, but that doesn't mean we give up. We have other tools at our disposal to carry on detecting. The internet, for one. Let's start with Facebook and Instagram and then move on to other social media platforms. He slipped up once when he attacked you instead of Elise. He'll have slipped up somewhere else. We can take it in turns using my computer. I'll make us another drink and then we'll get started.'

'Got something,' Hamlet called, looking up from his computer screen. He'd been searching for almost an hour, while Alix ploughed through Hamlet's copy of the investigation file. She'd taken the piles of documents from Hamlet's desk and laid them out over the study floor. She was sitting cross-legged, surrounded by paper.

'What've you got?' she said, looking up.

'I couldn't find Nate's name on any of the social media sites, so if he is on any of them then he's probably using an alias. So, what I've done is focus on his parents. His personnel file says they both died fourteen years ago. If they both died in the same year, perhaps it was in an accident. When I typed in Nate's father's name, Joe Fox, I instantly got a couple of hits. The first was an article from the *Kingsbridge and Salcombe Gazette*, dated Tuesday the seventh of October 2008.' He read out, '*Firefighters made a tragic discovery yesterday evening following their attendance at a fire in a barn in Inner Hope. Two bodies were found in a burned-out car. The barn is located on property belonging to Joe Fox and his wife Kate, and the bodies are believed to be those of the owners. Detectives investigating the fire say it is too early to say whether foul play is involved or not.*'

'Interesting,' muttered Alix, sitting up straighter.

'Certainly is. This is a headline from the paper's weekly edition three days later, on the tenth of October: "*Love triangle surrounds tragic suicide of local couple*".'

Alix's eyebrows shot up. 'Juicy! Tell me more.'

'In a nutshell, it repeats some of the previous article, but confirms that the two bodies were found in a burned-out Jaguar belonging to Joe and Kate Fox. It says that "their deaths are being treated as suicide and murder." Apparently, Joe was found in the driving seat of his Jaguar, and his wife Kate was found laid out on the back seat. They found a tube had been fitted to the exhaust and put through into the back of the car. A post-mortem revealed that Kate had extensive head injuries. The article says how well-known and popular they were in the area, and then makes mention of police attending the couple's home just a few weeks earlier following reports of domestic violence. It goes on to say that it was believed that Joe had been involved in a relationship with another woman, although no name is given. And get this —' Hamlet paused, making sure he had Alix's full attention — 'Joe Fox was a funeral director. He owned Fox's Funeral Parlour in Salcombe.'

Alix's jaw dropped. 'What!'

Hamlet nodded. 'Now we know how Nate got the skills to embalm the five women. And how he managed to get hold of the chemicals to do it.'

'Christ! We need to let the DI know about this. This changes everything. It will probably get us reinstated so we can to continue following up the investigation.'

'It's a little late today,' Hamlet said, looking at his watch. 'Lauren's probably gone home by now. You can ring her tomorrow.' Stretching, he added, 'In the meantime, I'll make us something to eat while you look for anything else about Joe and Kate Fox. There should at least be something online about the inquest.'

While Hamlet prepared a meal of tempura chicken from the freezer and salad from the fridge, Alix searched the internet for more on Joe and Kate Fox. Disappointingly, she found only a short article about the inquest, which listed the verdict as 'murder and suicide by Joe Fox,' with a one-sentence response from Devon and Cornwall Police that they were not looking for anyone else in connection with the deaths. There was nothing more recent. Printing off the report, she closed down the computer and made her way into the lounge, where Hamlet was placing two plates of food on the dining table.

Hamlet had opened a bottle of white wine, which Alix eyed with enthusiasm. It had been a shit day and she needed a pick-me-up. 'Just what the doctor ordered,' she said, picking up a glass and taking a long drink.

'I got the prescription right, then?' he replied, sitting down.

The television was on in the background — it had been on all afternoon as they monitored the news — and as Hamlet picked up his knife and fork, he saw that the local news had started. He seized the remote control and quickly increased the volume.

Alix turned her head as a wide shot of MIT headquarters appeared. A young, dark-haired reporter was in the middle of the screen, the training centre and Major Incident Team workplace behind her.

*'Questions are being raised today in connection with what has been dubbed the 'corpse brides' case. We can reveal that letters have been received by numerous news outlets which indicate that police have arrested the wrong man for the murder of five young women found two weeks ago in a disused World War Two bunker near Sheffield. We have also learned that Dr Hamlet Mottrell, the forensic psychologist whose family was slain four years ago, is once again under the spotlight, having been appointed a detective in the homicide team investigating the murders committed by the so-called 'Wedding Killer'. Sources reveal that he and a colleague are currently suspended and under investigation over wrongdoings linked to the investigation. We have approached South Yorkshire Police for comment, but they have not yet responded…'*

'What did you just say about getting reinstated, Alix?' Hamlet said, lowering the volume on the television. He didn't want to hear any more. He'd suffered enough at the hands of the media four years ago, and now he'd become a target again. He pushed away his plate. Suddenly, he wasn't hungry anymore.

Hamlet had trouble getting to sleep. He contemplated handing in his notice, but then he told himself he'd been through worse and had come out a stronger person. He could do it again — ride out the storm — the media attack would only be short-term. By the end of the week, the journalists would have moved on to another story and he and Alix could get on with their lives.

After what seemed like hours, he finally dropped off to sleep. He was just entering a dream in which Nate appeared as a disfigured groom with one of his embalmed brides when he was jerked awake by a series of sharp barks. Hamlet let out a moan. Lucky barking in the middle of the night wasn't unusual, particularly when a fox wandered too close to the cabin, and for a few seconds he lay there, knowing the terrier would settle down the moment the predator scampered away. But the barking showed no signs of abating. He heard Alix come out of the spare room and hiss, 'What's the matter boy?' Hamlet raised himself up, switched on the bedside light and launched himself out of bed.

Quickly putting on his dressing gown, he made his way into the lounge. Alix had switched on the light. He was stopped in his tracks by the sight. She was wearing his late wife's pink dressing gown. Over the years Helen had brought many items of clothing to the cabin for their weekend retreats, and in spite of it being four years since her passing, he still hadn't the heart to dispose of them. He felt a lump in his throat.

As if reading his thoughts, Alix said, 'I found this in the wardrobe. I hope you don't mind? I heard Lucky barking and wondered what was up.'

Her anxious words broke the spell. Helen's ghost disappeared, leaving him looking at a bleary-eyed Alix, her brown sleep-tousled hair hanging over her shoulders.

Lucky was by the French doors, face up against the glass, the hairs on his neck standing. He was still barking and a sudden flashback invaded Hamlet's thoughts. Four years ago, the killer who had slain his family had found out where he lived, sneaked into the woods while he was out, and then lain in wait to finish him off, having failed the first time around. A local newspaper's crime correspondent had also trespassed into the woods that day in the hope of digging up more dirt against him, his intention being to doorstep Hamlet, who had at the time been the prime suspect in his family's murders. Hamlet had returned home to find the reporter tied to the chair in his study, his wrists slashed. Dead. The local paper's headline that day became the crime correspondent's final epitaph, and Hamlet had been detained on suspicion of killing him by none other than Detective Nathaniel Fox.

Hamlet was taking no chances. He grabbed the hand-axe beside the fireplace and told Alix to switch off the light. As the room was plunged into darkness, Hamlet froze, holding his breath, listening. A low growl reverberated in Lucky's throat. As Hamlet's eyes adjusted, he gazed out through the French doors. The wooden planks of the veranda shone in the moonlight. Beyond the balcony, he could make out the first few yards of the clearing before a wall of blackness prevented his eyes searching further.

'What is it?' Alix whispered.

'I'm not sure. He doesn't usually bark like this. Something has spooked him.'

For the next minute they stood in silence, peering through the French doors, but nothing untoward caught their attention. Seeing that the hackles along Lucky's back had begun to flatten, Hamlet broke the silence by saying, 'Whatever it was has gone.' Relaxing the axe to his side, he switched the light back on and headed for his study. 'Let's see if anything's on the CCTV.' Since the crime correspondent's murder, Hamlet had surrounded the cabin with cameras secreted inside nest boxes. It had given him peace of mind. The system was linked to a hard drive in his study and backed up on his computer, with a synchronised alert app on his phone. As he made his way around his desk, he saw a red light flashing on the management console. 'Somethings been captured,' he said, booting up his computer and switching on the screen. Within seconds he was loading up the cameras, ten segments appearing on his screen. He slowly rewound the time frame, pausing the action as a dark-clad figure suddenly appeared in the bottom left segment. 'There,' exclaimed Hamlet, jabbing a finger.

He clicked on the screen to blow up the picture. The time in the right-hand corner was registered as 03.32, and someone wearing a dark padded jacket and beanie hat had entered the clearing close to where they had parked their cars. Hamlet set the recording to play and he and Alix watched as the intruder appeared from the side of the cabin and crept tentatively towards both their vehicles. They skirted around each one, peering inside as they went, before stepping back and heading towards the front of the cabin. Just as the prowler reached the bottom step of the veranda, they came to an abrupt halt, turned sharply and then fled back the way they had come. A split second later, the clearing was lit up by light pouring out from the cabin.

'That's when Lucky barked and you switched on the light, Alix,' Hamlet said, freezing the shot.

'Can you take it back and freeze on their face?' Alix asked.

Hamlet rewound the footage and then pressed play again, pausing several times, but the best shot he had of the trespasser was a side one. Even zoomed in to capacity, the hat and padded collar of their jacket prevented any recognition.

'Reporter, I bet,' Hamlet muttered. He was relieved. The trespasser didn't remotely match the physique of his family's killer — too short and not stocky enough.

*Thank God*, he thought to himself. *He hasn't escaped.*

'Parasite,' Alix blurted, pulling her eyes from the screen and yawning.

Hamlet closed down his computer. 'I'll set the bear traps tomorrow,' he announced with a smirk and stepped towards the kitchen. 'I'll make us a drink. I don't know about you, but I'm not going to be getting much sleep now, that's for sure.'

# SIX

Hamlet got up at first light, dressed quietly and took Lucky out for a walk. For the first ten minutes, Hamlet prowled around the clearing, looking to see if his mysterious night visitor had dropped something which would identify who they were. Failing to find anything, he set off through the woods, Lucky trotting ahead and foraging among the undergrowth. Forty minutes later they returned to the cabin and were greeted by the smell of frying bacon. Making his way into the kitchen, Hamlet found Alix forking rashers in a pan. She was dressed in her blue work slacks and a white blouse, her hair wet from her shower.

'Perfect timing,' she said, turning to look at him. 'Hope you don't mind — I got some bacon out of the freezer. I thought I'd make us a buttie before we started our day.'

'Just what I need. The way to a man's heart.' He slipped off his body warmer and hung it up, and then went to the sink to wash his hands. Drying them, he said, 'I've had a look round to see if I could find out who our visitor was, but they've not left any clues. It's my bet it was a reporter, probably from the local rag. They know where I live, after what happened to their crime reporter. Anyway, I've got some bird scarers tucked away that I bought ages ago. I'm going to set them around the cabin. If nothing else, it'll scare the shit out of them if they come snooping around again.'

While Hamlet fed and watered Lucky, Alix loaded the bacon into bread rolls and brewed them both a coffee. They took their breakfast outside and ate together at the table on the veranda, the early morning sunshine already warming the front of the cabin.

'This is lovely,' said Alix, tipping back her head in the early morning sunshine. There wasn't a cloud in the sky.

'We can work outside if you want? The internet signal is usually good out here,' Hamlet responded.

'That sounds like a great idea. I have my laptop in the boot. Do you want to carry on looking at the internet? I'd like to go back over the original missing reports for Nate's five victims. See if there's anything of note prior to their disappearance.'

Clearing away the breakfast things, Hamlet dragged his coffee table out onto the veranda, where Alix spread out the documents she wanted. Meanwhile, he worked at the table, booting up Alix's laptop. After a quick search, he found a few more articles relating to the deaths of Joe and Kate Fox from other local Devon newspapers and freesheets, but they were merely rewrites of what he had already read. He therefore began to Google, and found himself looking at a true-crime blog by someone called LittleMissMarple. It concerned the mysterious disappearance of a young woman named Olivia Kimble and immediately grabbed his attention thanks to the headline of the latest post, which was entitled *'Yorkshire Detective Serial Killer?'* It had been written a day ago. He opened it up and began reading.

*Today I received information from our regular guest blogger SalcombeCrimeGuy about a series of killings in Yorkshire that might prove to be a vital lead in discovering what happened to Livvy Kimble, who disappeared in 2008. I've learned from him that the bodies of five women, all in their early twenties, were recently discovered in an old World War II bunker near Sheffield, dressed as brides. They were murdered by a man the press have dubbed the 'Wedding Killer'. You would be forgiven for thinking that this is the stuff of fiction, but when I tell you that the killer is none other than a local detective, you must think again. And if you are asking yourself why I'm relating this story about a series of murders that occurred hundreds of miles away, it is because it's my understanding that the detective is the same Nathaniel Fox whose parents, Joe and Kate Fox, were found dead in their burned-out car in the garage of their home at Inner Hope just four months after the disappearance of 16-year-old Livvy, to whom this blog site is dedicated. And although there is nothing to suggest Nathaniel was involved in his parents' deaths (an inquest ruled that Joe killed his wife, and then killed himself by fitting a pipe from the exhaust into his car, during which it caught fire) he was one of the people interviewed by detectives following their deaths, and before that he was also interviewed by police during the search for Livvy, as he was among a group of people seen with Livvy on the night she vanished. The arrest of Nathaniel Fox now takes the mysterious disappearance of Olivia Kimble, 14 years ago, to a whole new level. You can be sure I will be following and reporting on what happens with the police investigation into the 'Wedding Killer', so keep tuning in to my blog. My thanks once again to SalcombeCrimeGuy for bringing this to my attention. If you want to learn more about The Mysterious Disappearance of Olivia Kimble, then listen to my recent podcast or follow the link to my blog.*

Hamlet clicked on the link. There was a whole raft of blogs about Olivia Kimble and he started to go through them, starting with the most recent. An hour later his eyes landed on the very first blog piece, written in 2008. As he read it, he got a tingling sensation that made the hairs on the back of his neck stand up.

*12th August 2008*
*It's four days since anyone saw my best friend, Livvy. This morning the sun is quite warm with only a light breeze drifting in from the sea. I am*

*standing on the cliffs above Hope Cove, watching a line of police scouring the path to the ancient remains of the Iron Age fort on Bolt Tail, the place Livvy said she was going to on Friday night. I feel empty. I was with her on Friday when she told me she was going to a party up there, and asked me if I'd go with her, but I couldn't. I'd promised Mum I'd be back before twelve. Now I wish I had gone, because I would have known what happened to her. Might have been able to prevent her vanishing. I say that because it's deeply suspicious that Livvy went off anywhere without telling anyone. In spite of her impulsiveness, she was also cautious. She would only have gone to the party if she had known who she was going with. And it must have been with someone who was at the pub on Friday. It was packed and there were many tourists there, a lot of them young, like us, but I never noticed her taking much interest in any of them and that must mean she went off with someone local. That's the scary thing about all this. It's more than likely that I know who is responsible for her going missing. I know people reading this will think I'm jumping to conclusions, but I know Livvy and she would not have gone anywhere with someone she didn't know. I've tried ringing her mobile and so have her mum and dad, as well as the police. But they say her phone is switched off. If anyone reading this has seen Livvy since 11.30pm last Friday, please tell the police. Keep following my blog for updates.*

Below the post was a photograph of the missing sixteen-year-old. Staring back at Hamlet was a slim teenager with black hair and heavy make-up. She was dressed in gothic clothing. Hamlet moved back to the blog and continued reading.

*14th August 2008*
*It's been six days since Livvy disappeared. I understand that a holidaying couple out walking their dog up on Bolt Tail late on Friday night saw the glow from a fire down below them. Police have confirmed they have found the remnants of a fire on the beach and will now be talking to everyone*

*who was at the pub last Friday. Who are you guys partying on the beach? Did you see Livvy? One of you must know what's happened to her. Everyone is under suspicion. Come forward if you've nothing to hide. If anyone knows who these people are, please contact the police. We all miss you, Livvy. Keep following my blog for updates.*

Hamlet let out a loud breath, causing Alix to look up. Leaning back, he said, 'Alix, you need to read this.'

Setting aside her paperwork, Alix pulled her chair up next to his and turned the laptop to get a better view. Hamlet clicked back to the first blog piece from 2008, watching Alix's facial expression as she read.

She finished reading and shot him a questioning look. 'So? What's the relevance of this?'

Hamlet scrolled quickly down the list of blog posts, stopping at LittleMissMarple's most recent post featuring Nathaniel Fox. Pointing to it, he said, 'Now read this.'

Alix read it quickly.

'See the relevance now?'

'Crikey. Yes. How did you find this?'

'Just played around with the keywords from the newspaper articles about Joe and Kate Fox, and where they lived, and this blog post popped up. It runs to dozens and dozens of posts, mainly about this missing girl, Olivia Kimble, and makes for very interesting reading.'

'Have you read them all?'

'Not all of them. There's quite a few. I've read the early ones from August 2008, when Olivia went missing. There's a long thread about her disappearance and police involvement in the early stages of the investigation. It appears that Olivia was the blogger's best friend. She spent the best part of eighteen months — in 2008 and 2009 — writing about the circumstances of her friend's disappearance and how anxious she was to find her. Much of it documents her feelings and thoughts, but she did a great job of keeping Olivia's disappearance in the spotlight. The media in Devon latched onto it and regurgitated various stories to keep her disappearance in the headlines. But then information dried up and the investigation stalled. This blogger continued to post during the intervening years and it was the last post, the one featuring Nathaniel, that led me to LittleMissMarple. And as you've just read, it seems Nate's no stranger to our blogger, nor to Olivia Kimble. She's certainly made the link regarding his parents' deaths, and I think I know how. When I found the newspaper article about Joe and Kate Fox, I looked on Google Earth to see if I could find the location of their house. It took me to a place called Inner Hope, and it's only a stone's throw from Hope Cove, which is where Olivia Kimble disappeared. I've worked out the dates and in August 2008, when Olivia disappeared, Nate would have been seventeen and, I'm guessing, still living with his parents, because their deaths weren't until October that year. He was a year older than Olivia. What's the bet they were at school together?'

'Wow. This is dynamite. The first blog mentioned that Olivia had gone to a party on the night she disappeared, and according to the most recent one, posted yesterday, Nate was interviewed by police because he was part of a group of people seen with her on the night she disappeared. This certainly confirms he knew her. Do any of the other posts directly mention Nate?'

'No. Only that last one. The blogger later posts about the police questioning local people, but she doesn't point the finger at anyone in particular.'

'Is there anything that fits in with what we know about Nate's victims?'

'You mean the stalking, the wedding invites they received before they were abducted? No. Nothing like that. But these posts have certainly thrown new light on Nate's background. My gut feeling from reading them is that we could well have found one of his first victims here.'

Alix gave him a curious look. 'You just said "one of his first victims". Are you saying there could be more?'

Taking a deep breath, he said, 'The first post in 2008 tells us that Olivia was invited to a party near some ancient remains on Bolt Tail, which are cliffs at the end of Hope Cove. Well, in the second post, written six days after Olivia went missing, the blogger makes reference to a couple out walking their dog up on Bolt Tail on the night Olivia was last seen. They saw the glow of a fire down below, and that sparked a police search where remnants of a fire were found on the beach. What's interesting about that find is that in another post the blogger states that "*there were no signs of any partying at the location. No traces of drink, or food, or even cigarette butts left behind.*" She writes: "*the place had been cleaned up of evidence.*" Follow-up posts touched on more personal details about Olivia; from those I've learned that she worked at the Hope and Anchor pub in Hope Cove. Probably clearing tables and serving food, given her age. LittleMissMarple also worked there, and they were both at work on the Friday evening Olivia disappeared. Olivia was invited to a party and asked her to go, but LittleMissMarple had promised her mum she'd go straight home that night. There is no mention of who invited Olivia. There is a hint the group may be local, but she never directly names anyone.'

Hamlet paused, then continued. 'As a matter of course the police searched the pub and outbuildings, and the beach.

LittleMissMarple also mentions that local sex offenders were questioned — she'll have picked that up from the media articles covering Olivia's disappearance. As you know, it's standard procedure with missing teenagers.' He paused again. 'Two months after Olivia's disappearance, her father, who conducted his own search, apparently found one of Olivia's Doc Marten boots in a hedgerow.'

Hamlet reached over to Alix's laptop, changed the screen to Google Maps, brought up the map of Hope Cove, and circled a finger over a piece of promontory headland at the end of the cove called Bolt Tail. 'It was somewhere around here. His find triggered another police search, and two days later they found Olivia's T-shirt hidden beneath a hedgerow bordering a farmer's field three quarters of a mile inland. More searches were made in woodland that skirted a place called Inner Hope to the top of Bolt Tail, and this is where things get interesting.'

After a couple of seconds silence, Alix said, 'Come on then, spit it out. It's like listening to one of those audio dramas, where they leave you on a cliff-hanger.'

Hamlet let out a short burst of laughter. 'Just checking I've got your attention, that's all.' He closed down Google Maps and brought up LittleMissMarple's blog posts. Selecting one, he clicked it open and said, 'Read this.'

Alix eyed the screen.

*20th August 2008*

*Over the past week the police have searched the woods at the top of Bolt Tail and the fields after Livvy's dad found one of her boots. They found her T-shirt and yesterday they found a backpack containing more items of clothing, but it isn't Livvy's. That got me wondering whom it might belong to, and I think I know the answer. Two months ago, a policeman asked Livvy and I if we knew anything about Harriet Swann, a barmaid at the*

*Hope and Anchor who had been reported missing by her parents in Exeter. Livvy and I would chat with her during our shifts. She told us she was 18 and had just finished her exams and was doing some travelling before going to uni in September. She was camping in the fields near Bolberry, and me and Livvy went up there a couple of times. I remember her telling us that she'd met one of the local lads and might be staying around a bit longer than she thought. We asked who he was, but she just laughed and said she was sworn to secrecy. That was the last we saw of Harriet. The Thursday of her third week, she didn't turn up for work. She didn't come in on the Friday either and so that Saturday me and Livvy went up to where she was camping. We found the patch where her tent had been, but no tent. We assumed she must have fallen out with the lad she'd met and had either gone back home to Exeter or moved on to somewhere else. I've contacted the police at Exeter and Harriet is still missing. Is Harriet's disappearance linked to Livvy's disappearance? If anyone reading this knows anything about Harriet Swann, please respond. Keep following my blog for updates.*

Alix's eyes darted from the screen to Hamlet. 'This is incredible. Two missing girls from 2008. Both from the same place, Hope Cove in Devon, where Nate lived when he was younger. This blog is a goldmine.'

Hamlet nodded. 'I think so too. I'm going to read the rest of the posts and then see if I can find any more information about Olivia Kimble and Harriet Swann in the media. Then I'm going to send a message to LittleMissMarple. We really need to talk to her.'

Hamlet continued going through LittleMissMarple's blog, this time focusing on the posts about 18-year-old Harriet Swann's disappearance, many of them linking to newspaper articles, which he steadily combed through. Slowly moving through the first half dozen articles, Hamlet noticed that the structure of the prose was a lot more formal and he guessed LittleMissMarple was constructing them with the aid of media feeds. Nevertheless, they were still useful, and by the time he had finished reading he had formed a picture in his mind of what Harriet was like as a person, together with a chronology of her time in Hope Cove prior to her going missing. It also helped that a photograph of Harriet had been displayed beneath the first article. The 18-year-old had long dark hair and wore a faded denim jacket over a T-shirt. He caught Alix's attention with a wave of his hand. 'Can I disturb you a minute?'

Alix lowered the documents she had been reading. 'Got something?'

'I believe I have. I've just read through all the posts relating to Harriet Swann and I think LittleMissMarple may have something. Before I tell you, take a look at Harriet's photo.' Hamlet turned the laptop towards Alix. 'See the likeness to the five victims from the bunker? Do you remember I told you before we found their bodies that the person who abducted them had a type?'

'Yes,' Alix replied slowly. 'I see what you mean. She does have a likeness to the others. And I'm guessing that she's still missing?'

Hamlet nodded. 'I can't find anything on the internet to say she's been found. The newspaper articles state that she was reported missing on the ninth of June 2008 by her mother, who hadn't heard from her since the fourth, which was a Friday. And one of LittleMissMarple's posts mentions that Harriet didn't turn up for work on the Thursday, which was the fifth of June.'

'And Olivia Kimble went missing in August. Two months later?'

'Yes. If you recall, she was last seen at work by LittleMissMarple on Friday the twelfth of August.'

'Anything significant about Harriet's disappearance?'

Hamlet shook his head. 'No. Her disappearance was covered by the Exeter *Express and Echo*, where she lived. And that was only a couple of paragraphs. There was a bit more in *The Exeter Daily* online blog, but not much. Apparently, the police didn't initially believe she had come to any harm, and so they didn't prioritise the case. It was only after they found her backpack whilst searching for Olivia Kimble that any real effort was made to try and find her. And that was thanks to LittleMissMarple, who raised her suspicions with Exeter Police. Harriet's mum told the press that her daughter was a confident young woman who had gone to Glastonbury Festival with friends during the previous year, 2007. She'd enjoyed it so much that she had arranged to do the same thing in 2008. On this occasion she had decided to go backpacking in Cornwall and Devon first, before catching up with her friends at Glastonbury and then heading back home ready to start university in Exeter. It appears Hope Cove was her first port of call. She had saved up some money for her trip, but got the job doing bar work at the Hope and Anchor pub to supplement her savings. We know from LittleMissMarple that she'd set up her tent at nearby Bolberry. The newspapers say that she kept in touch with her mother regularly right up until the night she went missing. When her mum didn't hear from her for a few days, she contacted the police. We know from LittleMissMarple's blog that the police made enquiries at the pub, but it appears that they assumed she'd moved on and was heading up to Glastonbury. That's all I can find out without contacting Exeter police direct. By the time her backpack had been found, she'd been missing for two months. The trail had gone cold.

'Both Harriet and Olivia are still officially listed as missing. I'm going to contact Exeter police and see if I can get a copy of Harriet's missing persons report. I also think now is the time to let Lauren know what we've found.'

'I think you're right,' Alix agreed with a nod.

# SEVEN

At 6 foot 4 inches tall and weighing in at 17 stone, Detective Superintendent David Butler had a presence that demanded respect. His authority came not just from his intimidating size, but also from working at the sharp end of policing for twenty-six years and with several commendations to boot. His latest role was head of the Professional Standards Department, investigating crooked cops, which he took very seriously.

This morning he was meeting with DCI Jackson and DI Simmerson at MIT headquarters to discuss the so-called 'Wedding Killer' investigation. The previous day he had read through all material pertinent to the inquiry and had prepared a list of questions he expected to be answered. The meeting had been fixed for 8 a.m. sharp, but as usual he had arrived early, letting himself into the building with his high-level swipe card and making his way to Lauren's office to await the two senior officers' arrival. Slipping off his suit jacket and making sure the ID on his lanyard was facing the right way, he seated himself at the small conference table and took out the paperwork from his bag, adding his journal and fountain pen. Then, folding his arms, he settled back in his seat facing the door. He always liked to monitor the look he was greeted with by his *clients*. Their response determined how he set the next few hours of discussion. At ten minutes to eight he heard voices coming down the corridor. As the DCI and DI entered he saw their surprised expressions, followed quickly by Lauren Simmerson's cheerful, 'You're early, Sir. Can I get you a coffee?'

Lauren had her own coffee machine, and she brought three lattes over to the conference table. After passing them around, she made herself comfortable next to her DCI. She had brought her own journal and pen to the table and opening it to a fresh page, she wrote the date at the top left before setting down her pen.

Taking a sip of his coffee, Butler began, 'As you know, the Police and Crime Commissioner has agreed to another force coming in to review the work your team did on the investigation into the murders of five women whose bodies were found two weeks ago in a disused bunker in Low Bradfield, which resulted in the arrest of Detective Nathaniel Fox, who has now been charged and detained for further questioning. I'm here to let you know that yesterday it was determined that that review will be carried out by Greater Manchester, and alongside that my department has been asked to look at the conduct of two officers who were closely involved in that investigation.'

'DS Rainbow and DC Mottrell,' Jackson responded.

Butler nodded.

Lauren said, 'I've known DS Rainbow for a number of years. She's a very good detective. One of my best officers. She is scrupulously thorough in her work.'

'That's as may be,' Butler returned, 'but I have been asked to investigate allegations made against her by Nathaniel Fox's solicitor.'

'Can I ask what those allegations are?' asked Jackson.

'Of course, but I must ask that what I tell you both, you keep to yourselves. No regulation notices have been served yet and our investigation is in the very early stages. We've also had to refer it to the Independent Office for Police Conduct for investigation due to the nature of the allegations. In a nutshell, Nathaniel Fox is alleging that DS Rainbow and DC Mottrell, or someone else, planted incriminating evidence at his home leading to his arrest.'

'And with respect, Sir, that's bullshit,' Lauren exclaimed. 'I know how that evidence was obtained and I know it wasn't planted.'

'Were you there, DI? When it was discovered?'

'No, but…'

Butler held up a hand. 'Well, in that case, you know you can't support your comment. You more than anyone should know about jumping to conclusions. I have been given a job to do and I can assure you I will do it thoroughly. If it is "bullshit", as you claim, then I will find out.' He picked up his pen. 'You say you've known DS Rainbow a number of years?'

'Yes. She's been a member of my team for almost five years. She is dedicated to her job, and as I said, an excellent detective. I supported her promotion to sergeant. She came in the top ten of her board and has been the sergeant of Syndicate One for four years.'

'I understand she investigated the murders of Dr Mottrell's family four years ago?'

Lauren nodded. 'Yes, Sir. That was her first job following promotion. As you probably know, Hamlet was our main suspect for a long time. That was until he discovered that the murder of a young woman in Derbyshire had been committed by the same man who killed his family. A patient who escaped from the secure unit where he worked as a forensic psychiatrist. Hamlet helped track him down and arrest him.'

'Yes, I've learned all that from the information I've gathered. I understand that DS Rainbow was with Dr Mottrell on the night Benson was arrested?'

'That's right. Benson confessed to Hamlet about the murders. He tried to kill Hamlet, but Alix rescued him. Benson was arrested by uniform after Alix put out an emergency call.'

Butler gave an understanding nod. 'DS Rainbow wasn't present when he got that confession?'

'No.' Lauren let the word out slowly. 'Where are you taking this, Sir?'

'Nathaniel Fox's solicitor believes that DS Rainbow has been duped by Dr Mottrell. That she got too close to him during that investigation and allowed herself to be swayed by what he told her.'

'Now, just a minute, Sir. I led that investigation and was present when Hamlet presented Alix with the evidence that led us to Benson.'

'That's as may be, but am I correct when I say that you didn't see *how* he obtained that evidence?'

Lauren glanced quickly at Jackson before returning her gaze to Butler. 'No, I didn't. But nothing about his actions made me suspicious.'

'I'm sure they didn't. And everything may be above board. Dr Mottrell is probably innocent and Benson killed his family, but Nathaniel Fox alleges you got it wrong. That Dr Mottrell is the real killer. He took you all in by feeding you false evidence. He also alleges that Dr Mottrell murdered the five women found in the bunker. That he planted evidence that led you on a false trail to Fox.'

'With all due respect, Sir, that's nonsense. Nate is trying to detract attention from himself by blaming someone else.'

'And with all due respect, DI Simmerson, that's my job to find out. Benson didn't confess. Am I right?'

'He refused to talk during his interviews.'

'So, we do only have Dr Mottrell's word that Benson confessed to him?'

'Well, yes.'

'That's why it's necessary to investigate. Nathaniel Fox is alleging Dr Mottrell killed his family for money and then concocted an elaborate plot to blame James Benson, a former psychiatric patient of his. Dr Mottrell received over a million pounds following the death of his parents, from the GP practice his father owned and the sale of the family house. He also received a further four hundred thousand pounds from his wife's life insurance and the sale of their home following her death. That's a lot of money. Worth killing for?'

'I've known people who'd kill for less. But let me reassure you, during the investigation into Hamlet, both as the SIO and corroborating detective for Alix, I got to know Hamlet and I'm confident we got the right person.'

'I hear what you are saying, but are you aware that Dr Mottrell has being seeing a psychiatrist for the last four years?'

'Well, that's not surprising, given what he's gone through. His entire family was murdered,' Lauren responded.

'Granted. But it's more than counselling for bereavement. He's disclosed that he's suffered blackouts and on a couple of occasions when he's come round, he's discovered injuries to his knuckles that he couldn't explain. He's been diagnosed with something called dissociative fugue. It's a behavioural disorder brought on by trauma. That is very worrying, don't you think?'

'I didn't know that. But I have to say that I've not seen him with any injuries and not noticed anything untoward in his demeanour. His performance during his first case has been exemplary,' said Lauren.

'That's as may be, but it's my understanding that this disorder is not present all the time. It can come and go. I've

57

also learned that Dr Mottrell has been visiting James Harry Benson in his secure unit for the past three months.' Butler paused to let his words sink in.

Lauren shook her head. 'I wasn't aware of that,' she replied.

Butler leaned forward, interlocking his fingers. 'It seems to me that Dr Mottrell is holding things back that he should be mentioning. He's keeping secrets that do not sit comfortably with me. In addition, we received this this morning.'

Butler dipped into his briefcase and extracted an evidence wallet that he placed on the table, turning it so Lauren and Jackson could see. The clear plastic wallet contained a typewritten note. It looked similar to the one that had been placed under the windscreen wipers of the police car two days previously.

They read the text.

*It's me again, Chief Pig. Aren't you listening to what I said in my first note? Clearly not. Well, let me spell it out for you. YOU HAVE THE WRONG MAN. It's me you are after, and to prove it I'll give you a clue. A big clue. I smothered those five women by putting a suicide bag over their heads. And each of the bitches deserved it. And just to keep you on your toes, there will be another if you don't take me seriously.*

*The Wedding Killer Lol.*

Butler returned the note to his briefcase. 'I think you'll agree that there is information in this note that only the killer knows. And it definitely didn't come from Nathaniel Fox, because he's been in the cells since his arrest. This note clearly highlights that there is a possibility you have arrested the wrong person, and Fox's accusations leave me with no other option but to look at Dr Mottrell's involvement in the arrest. And I'm afraid that also includes DS Rainbow's actions. I need to cover all bases.'

From her office door, Lauren watched Detective Superintendent Butler pass through the security door, making sure it closed behind him before closing her own door. Jackson was still seated at the conference table, his head resting in his hands.

'What do you make of that?' she said, taking her place back at the table.

'He's raised some very serious issues about Hamlet's state of mind. What did he say — behavioural disorder, injuries to his hands that he couldn't explain, blackouts?' Jackson straightened. 'Did you have any inkling about this?'

'I knew he'd been seeing a psychiatrist about his family's murders, but nothing about the blackouts and unexplained injuries or the psychological disorder. I really had no idea about that.' She sighed. 'This is bad. Butler seems to think that Hamlet has pulled the wool over our eyes, that not only could he be the "Wedding Killer", but that he might in fact be responsible for his own family's murders. You were there every day of that investigation, Karl; you saw the same evidence as me. Did you ever get the inkling that Hamlet had killed his family?'

'Not at the time, Lauren. No. But it's something we're going to have to think about. Superintendent Butler's right about the confession from Benson. Only Hamlet was there when it was supposedly made. Alix was out of earshot. The other thing I don't like is that Hamlet has been visiting Benson. Why? Is it to keep Benson quiet?'

'It's Alix I feel sorry for. She's caught up in the middle of this through no fault of her own.'

'Alix can look after herself. We know that. If she thinks for one minute there's something dodgy about Hamlet, she'll suss it out and get to the bottom of it. Mark my words.'

'Maybe I should just give her the heads up.'

# EIGHT

It was cool but comfortable in the woods. Hamlet was on an extended morning walk with Lucky, thinking through what he and Alix had uncovered the previous day. Following his discovery of the blog, Alix had tried calling Lauren to pass on what they had unearthed, but each time the DI's phone had gone to voicemail. When she hadn't returned her calls by 6.30 p.m., they had called it a day and Alix had gone home, telling him she'd try to ring Lauren again later in the evening. At 10 o'clock, when Hamlet not heard back from Alix, he'd gone to bed.

An hour later, he had just returned from the walk when he felt his phone vibrate. Pulling it from his pocket, he saw that it was the DI. *Just the person.* He greeted her with a friendly, 'Morning, boss,' but before he could say anything else she interrupted. For the best part of two minutes he listened without saying a word, and when she finished he simply replied, 'Okay,' and ended the call. For several seconds he stared at his mobile, his mind and body suddenly numb. He hadn't been expecting that call. His thoughts raced while he grappled with the magnitude of what she had said. It was the same feeling he'd had four years ago, when he'd woken up in a hospital bed and Alix had told him that his wife and unborn child were dead, as were his adoptive parents. And that he was being arrested for their murders. He felt sick.

Taking a deep breath to curb the nausea, he suddenly thought of Alix and immediately rang her. For what seemed an eternity, there was no answer and he was preparing to leave a message when she came on the line. All she said was, 'Hamlet,' but the despondency in her tone told him she'd had the same phone call from the DI.

'I'm guessing you've had a phone call from Lauren?' he said.

'Yes. She told me we're under investigation. That some serious issues have been raised and they could take some time to resolve. She wouldn't tell me what. That's not like her. This is not good. Not good at all. To be honest I don't know if I can take any more of this, Hamlet.' She broke into a sob and ended the call.

Hamlet instantly hit redial. It went to voicemail. He hung up and tried again. No answer. He left a message: 'Alix, please ring me back.' Suddenly he was worried. She'd had a lot to contend with these past six months. She'd told him of the guilt she felt at not visiting her unwell father, who was undergoing treatment for bowel cancer, because she could not face going to her parents' house, the scene of her rape. Added to that had been the two back-to-back complex investigations she'd headed up following her promotion to detective sergeant. They had been physically and mentally exhausting. Finding the body of her friend Elise had taken its toll. He had seen the look on her face when she had realised who she was looking at, and he had seen the change in her demeanour since, in spite of the steely front she'd put on to disguise her feelings. He had tried to get her to open up, but she hadn't wanted to talk about it. She'd found it difficult to believe that the person who had raped her as a teenager and killed Elise was Nathaniel Fox, her work colleague and friend. And now this. It was a lot to handle, even with Alix's training and experience. Spurred into action, he dashed into the cabin, snatched up his car keys, jumped into his Range Rover and tore down the track to the main road.

His heart racing as fast as the car, Hamlet sped down the motorway, overtaking dangerously and finally screeching up sharply outside Alix's Victorian townhouse half an hour later. Jogging up the steps to the door, he rapped loudly. No answer. He hammered again and called her name through the letterbox, then crouched down and peered through into the hallway. When she still didn't appear, he tried the handle. It was unlocked. That surprised him. Alix was so security-conscious. He opened it cautiously and stepped into the carpeted hallway, calling out her name and trying to suppress the urgency in his voice. To his left was the lounge and at the end of the hallway was the kitchen. Both rooms were empty. He returned to the bottom of the stairs and looked up.

'Alix,' he called.

Still no response.

He took the stairs two at a time, his heart thumping. He hoped she hadn't done anything stupid. At the top he heard sobbing coming from the bathroom. *Thank God.* The door was ajar. He pushed it open slowly. Alix was sitting on the floor, her back against the bathtub, legs drawn up to her chest. Blood was dripping from her thighs onto the floor and her hands were covered in it. Beside her was a sharp kitchen knife.

Hamlet's head span. *She's cut herself again.*

Months ago, in a drunken unguarded moment, Alix had told him how, following the rape, she had self-harmed, slicing chunks into her inner thighs. Her way, she said, of cleansing herself of the degradation she felt. She hoped that the ugly scars would put off any other man from doing it again. He had never seen the scars, but he could see them now. She had opened a few of them up, as well as making fresh ones. She gazed up at him with tear-filled eyes. The steeliness he knew was gone. In its place was a fragile, fractured look. Hamlet grabbed a towel from the rail. 'Oh, Alix, what have you done?' he said, bending down and pressing the towel against her legs to stem the flow of blood.

'I've had enough, Hamlet,' she sobbed. 'I've given everything to this job, and they treat me like this. Like *I'm* the criminal. They put me on gardening leave — their way of telling me I'm suspended. For fuck's sake.' She let out a wail.

Hamlet took hold of her and pulled her close. He could feel the heavy sobs racking her body. 'This is not your fault, Alix.'

'They're saying Nate might not be the killer. That someone else killed Elise and the others. That we got it wrong. Nate's solicitor is applying for bail.' She pulled herself back from Hamlet and looked into his eyes. 'We didn't get it wrong, did we? It was Nate who did this? And Nate who attacked me?'

'There's only one way to find out,' Hamlet replied, holding her teary gaze. 'Now, let's get you cleaned up. We've got a job to do.'

After cleaning Alix up and patching her wounds — a couple of the cuts had required Steri-Strips — Hamlet had raided her fridge and made them both a sandwich. He had done his best to persuade Alix that their gardening leave was nothing more than procedure and not vindictiveness. 'You know Lauren. She has consistently backed you throughout your career, and I'm sure she's rooting for you right now.'

Alix smiled and, turning to him, she said, 'Thank you.'

'That's what friends are for.'

'Not for patching up detectives who self-harm. I mean it, Hamlet. You deserve a medal in my book.'

'I'm a doctor, don't forget. That's what friends who are doctors do.'

She leaned in and pecked him on the cheek. As she pulled back, she blushed. For a couple of seconds there was an uncomfortable silence between them, which Alix quickly broke by saying, 'I'll make us a drink and then I'll let you go. Lucky'll be missing you.'

She headed for the kitchen and Hamlet followed.

'I'm in no rush. Gardening leave, remember.'

That brought a laugh from Alix and eased the tension. 'Good bedside humour as well, Doc.'

In the kitchen she filled the kettle and took two mugs from the cupboard. Spooning in coffee, she said, 'Really, Hamlet, I'm okay now. This has brought me to my senses. Doing what I did is not going to change things.' She took milk from the fridge and poured a little into each mug, mixing the granules. 'I'll make us this and then you get yourself off. I'm going to catch up with some housework. I haven't had a moment these past few weeks, and now is the perfect opportunity.'

'Well, if you're sure.'

'I'm sure. Honestly, I'm fine. I really appreciate you being there for me and I'm sorted now. You get off and give that lovely pooch of yours some company. He'll be glad to have some time with you for a change.' The kettle boiled and she made the coffee. Handing him a mug, she continued, 'Have this and then leave me to get on with my cleaning. I've got a basketful of ironing, too. I'll ring you tonight. They haven't said we mustn't communicate with one another. What about lunch tomorrow?'

'That sounds good.'

'That's a date, then.'

That evening Hamlet conducted some more internet research, looking at any sites LittleMissMarple's blog had links with. These were mainly digital armchair detectives who blogged about people who had vanished in mysterious circumstances. Some were very creative with their theories, while others made spurious links to jailed serial killers, which had amused him. It struck him, however, that there were a lot of people online keeping missing persons' stories alive.

He printed off some of the posts and linked articles, assembling the paperwork into three piles: one with references to Harriet Swann, another for Olivia Kimble, and the third on other missing women mentioned by the armchair detectives that Hamlet didn't want to dismiss just yet. As he looked at the three piles he realised there was a lot of work to do. His head had started to throb from the earlier stressful incident with Alix, and he decided to call it a day. He would start again in the morning, when fresh.

Before powering off his computer, he checked his emails to see if LittleMissMarple had replied to the one he'd sent her the previous evening. She hadn't. He composed another, this time using his police email address, hoping that would grab her attention and encourage a reply.

# NINE

Hamlet stretched and yawned. Sunlight poured in through the window and he instantly felt invigorated. The last couple of nights he'd slept badly and had had to drag himself out of bed in the morning. But last night sleep had caught up with him and he felt reenergised. He reached for his phone and activated the screen. The time was 07.34 and he saw that he had an email waiting.

It was from LittleMissMarple.

*From: LittleMissMarple@gmail.com*
*Subject: Harriet Swann & Olivia Kimble*
*Dear Detective Mottrell, my apologies for not answering your earlier email but I was nervous about replying because of all the hassles I've had since creating my blog, which I won't go into in this email. You mention that the disappearance of Harriet Swann and my friend Livvy is of interest to you because of a case you are working on and that you would like to meet to discuss their disappearance. I would love to. I've waited so long to hear news like this. Are you able to come down to Devon?*

*Regards*
*Erin Scott*

Hamlet pushed himself up. LittleMissMarple now had a name. Erin Scott. He re-read her email. Why couldn't he go to Devon? After all, he was on gardening leave until further notice, and no one had told him that he was confined to South Yorkshire. And Erin wasn't to know his visit would be in a non-official capacity, so long as he didn't mention it. Propping himself up against his pillow, he composed his reply.

By the time he had showered and dressed, Erin had sent another email. It was short and to the point, telling him she couldn't wait to meet and share her information with him. She provided her phone number for him to call when he arrived.

Flinging open the French doors to let in the warmth and freshness of the summer morning, Hamlet made himself tea and toast and took it out to the veranda, where he ate breakfast watching the birds in the trees and feeling galvanised. Why shouldn't he speak with Erin? Work didn't know about her existence, nor about Harriet Swann and Olivia Kimble, and their possible link to Nate Fox. Only he and Alix knew. The thought of Alix sparked an idea. He picked up his mobile and rang her.

'I've not woken you, have I?' he said when she answered.

'Yes, you have,' she moaned. 'I was having the best sleep I've had in ages.'

'Well, sleepy-head, I won't apologise because I have a proposal for you. How do you fancy going away?'

'What do you mean, going away?'

'Going away, as in a holiday. Well, not exactly a holiday. More a busman's holiday.'

'Hamlet, we're already in enough trouble.'

'Well, if you don't want to hear what I have to say, I'll go to sunny Devon on my own.'

'Devon! You've got something?' She suddenly sounded wide awake.

'Not exactly, but it's looking promising. LittleMissMarple has returned my email. Her name is Erin Scott. She wants to talk and has asked if I can go down there.'

'Oh, okay.'

'You up for it? Work doesn't need to know. If they contact you, just tell them you've gone away for a break.'

'And what happens if we find something that work needs to know about?'

'We can discuss that if it happens.'

'I'm not sure, Hamlet. I don't want to make the situation worse.'

Sensing her reticence, he said, 'Oh, come on, where's your sense of adventure? What's the saying — fortune favours the brave.'

'There's brave and there's reckless.'

Hamlet sniggered. 'Since when have you erred on the side of caution?'

'Since they suspended me.'

'Gardening leave. Not suspension. I'll take full responsibility. It's my idea, after all.'

Alix was quiet for several seconds. Then she said, 'Oh, go on then. Bugger it. I could do with a holiday. I'll blame you if it goes belly-up.'

'Great! I'll find us somewhere to stay and get back to you.'

Hamlet ended the call.

Hamlet awoke feeling nervous but excited. What he was about to embark on was highly contentious and could cause him to lose his new career; however, given his and Alix's present predicament, he could see no other way of finding out if Erin Scott's blogs had any relevance to their investigation. It was too good an opportunity to miss. If everything she had published was merely conjecture with no hard facts, they could thank her and then spend the remainder of their stay in Devon playing the role of tourists, which would provide the perfect cover if word got back to Lauren. It was a gamble worth pursuing.

As he traipsed to the kitchen to make himself a mug of tea, he spotted Alix sitting at the table on the veranda, Lucky lying at her feet, the pair of them taking in the sounds and smells of early morning. She had driven over with her bags the previous afternoon and slept in the spare room. She turned and smiled at him through the open French doors.

'Did I disturb you?' she asked.

He shook his head. 'No, I've got up to make myself a brew. Do you want one?'

'Coffee would be lovely. I'm just taking in the morning air. It's so peaceful here. You're so lucky.'

'I guess I am now. I didn't used to think that when I first came here, after what happened, but now I realise how fortunate I am waking up to this every day.' He made his way in to the kitchen, filled the kettle, switched it on and lined up two mugs. 'Still up for this?' he shouted over his shoulder.

Alix shouted back, 'What have we got to lose? As far as anyone needs to know, we're going on holiday. The fact that it's Devon, where Nate comes from, is neither here nor there. If they want to make something of it, they'll have to prove that what we're doing is against regulations.'

Hamlet chuckled to himself. 'I'm of the same mind. And if we don't turn anything up, then the break will do us both good. I've checked the forecast. We've got four days of glorious sunshine with the slim chance of thunderstorms by the end of the week, so it's even looking good for a couple of beach visits.' The kettle boiled and he made tea for himself and a coffee for Alix, taking the mugs out to the veranda. Plonking the drinks down on the table, he sat down in the vacant chair.

'You say you've got us a sea view?' she said, picking up her steaming mug and wrapping her hands around it.

'Yeah. The cottage looks great. Seventeenth century with a thatched roof. It's laid out so that the lounge and both bedrooms face the sea. We can wake up to the sound of the waves crashing on the beach.'

'Sounds absolutely perfect.'

'I've decided I'm not going to message Erin until we get there. I thought that when we arrive, we'd take a look around first. Get a feel for the place. You know, see what's what in terms of location — visit Bolt Tail and the area where Harriet Swann was camping before she went missing. I had another look on Google Maps yesterday afternoon and the two locations aren't far from one another — roughly a mile — so I thought we'd have a stroll around before we arrange to meet with Erin.'

'Sounds like you have it all in hand. We'll make a detective of you yet.' Alix let out a light laugh and took a sip of her coffee.

After a light breakfast of cereal and toast, they loaded up Hamlet's Range Rover, went for a quick stroll so that Lucky could get a toilet break in before the journey, and then, strapping the little dog into the back seat, they set off towards the motorway. At Michaelwood services they stopped to stretch their legs before continuing onwards, finally entering Devon four and a half hours after setting off.

They picked up the A38, passing Newton Abbot and Totnes, before again temporarily halting their journey in the town of Kingsbridge, where they decided to stock up on provisions. They found a small supermarket, a fresh fish shop and a family butcher, buying enough supplies for a week, as well as an Ordnance Survey map of South Devon.

The final leg of the journey was more challenging. The roads became narrower after leaving Kingsbridge. At several sections the B-roads were just thin strips of tarmac with steep sides of vegetation, and so constricted that, had it not been for passing points hewn into the verges, there would have been no means of passing oncoming vehicles. Thankfully, the roads were quiet and Hamlet only had to pull in twice before arriving at Hope Cove. Hamlet let out an exuberant 'Wow!' and gave Alix a quick smile as the village came into view. Whitewashed cottages were tucked tightly into the hillside that snaked down towards two small sandy beaches.

They came to a halt before a couple of thatched-roof cottages. To the left was the Hope and Anchor pub, where both Olivia Kimble and Harriet Swann had once worked. 'Fancy a drink before we find our cottage?' Hamlet said, turning to Alix.

'You read my mind. I'm parched.' Her eyes strafing the view before her, she added, 'This place is so beautiful. What a discovery. It's so off the beaten track that you wouldn't even know it existed.'

'I couldn't think of a better place to be holed up for the next week,' he replied, springing open his car door. 'Come on, we'll get a drink and some lunch and then find our cottage. It shouldn't be too hard to spot.'

# TEN

The Hope and Anchor pub was light and airy, its old interior given a contemporary look with pastel-painted walls of light grey and off-white. The bar was well stocked with local ales from St Austell Brewery. Hamlet ordered a beer while Alix chose a pear cider. Lucky was given a bowl of water. They were surprised at how busy the place was, it being off-peak. Most of the customers appeared to be tourists, judging by their shorts and T-shirts.

They grabbed one of the tables by the window, overlooking the courtyard, as a group of four vacated. It was cluttered with empty plates from a finished meal, and they piled them to one side and took the seats next to the window. From here they had a glimpse over the sea wall down to the beach, where the tide was out. Hamlet took the top off his beer, staring out across the cove. In the sunshine the receding waters sparkled green and blue. Already he could feel the stress of driving 300 miles, most of it busy motorway, leaving his body. 'Even if we come away with nothing but a week of fresh air and sunshine, it'll be worth the journey,' he said, mesmerised by the beauty of the location.

'I feel better already,' agreed Alix. 'And this is like nectar,' she added, holding up her glass. 'Cheers!'

Hamlet saw she was halfway down her cider already. 'Shall we get some food?' he suggested, picking up a menu. At a glance he could see that the lunchtime food was mainly of the pub-grub variety. 'Do you know what, I fancy fish and chips,' he said, laying down the menu. 'That's what you eat when you are at the seaside, isn't it?'

'I'll have the same. And another pint of this pear cider. It's gorgeous.'

Hamlet and Alix finished their meal, along with another drink, agreeing that they were glad they had chosen the fish and chips. The flaky white chunks of cod were encased in crisp, golden beer batter, and the chips had been triple-cooked. They settled the bill and left a tip. Once outside, they made their way across to the stone sea wall, peering over the edge to the beach below. Beyond the sandy beach, rows of jagged rocks led to the sea and to their left was a sizeable rocky outcrop with a cliff-face of roughly thirty feet.

Thinking out loud, Hamlet said, 'I'm sure the cove was bigger than this from looking at the map. Let's go for a stroll.' Lucky wagged his tail.

They set off along a narrow street that took them past a row of blue-, yellow- and cream-painted cottages, where the view opened up to reveal a second, much larger beach, at the end of which was a huge headland of dark rugged cliffs.

'This is what I remember seeing,' exclaimed Hamlet. 'I think those cliffs in front of us are Bolt Tail. It's up there where Olivia supposedly went to a party on the night she disappeared. Somewhere on top are the remains of an Iron Age fort. Fancy a stroll to go and have a look?'

'Not all the way up there, I don't. It looks a good steep climb, and I haven't got the shoes for it,' Alix replied, lifting up a foot to show Hamlet her ballet pumps. 'We can stroll along the beach to the bottom, if you like, but that's as far as I'll go.'

'Fair enough.'

As they dropped down to the beach, Hamlet noticed that the harbour wall dog-legged out to sea. Moored next to it was an array of small inflatable dinghies and sail boats. There was more activity on this beach; a number of people were taking paddle boards and surfboards out to sea.

The further they walked the wetter the sand became, so they slipped off their shoes and squelched on until they came to the headland. At the foot of the steep cliffs was a concrete jetty that led up to a large stone building. To the right of that a steep path with steps had been cut into the hillside. It wound its way upwards, disappearing into a bank of trees that looked like the beginnings of a wood. A signpost at the bottom of the steps informed them that Bolt Tail lay three quarters of a mile away.

Hamlet started up the jetty. 'It looks a fair old climb. I'm glad now you've got the wrong shoes on — I don't think I can face that walk today. We'll maybe look at it tomorrow, when we're fresh.' He looked around. 'Do you know, I believe this is where our cottage is. I remember in the blurb that it was near the lifeboat station, and this is the lifeboat station,' he announced, pointing to the large stone building. At the top of the jetty was a narrow road with more pastel-painted houses that appeared to wend their way to a wooded hillside that towered in the distance. 'This is Inner Hope. Nate used to live here with his parents. I wonder which was his house?'

'I'm sure Erin will know. We can get her to show us when we meet up,' Alix replied, taking in the view.

'And if I'm not mistaken, this is our cottage,' Hamlet proclaimed gleefully, pointing across the road towards a white-painted thatched cottage set in a reasonably large grassed garden on the corner. He quick-stepped across the narrow road, stopping at a five-bar gate set in a low stone wall. 'Yes, this is it. Wave Cottage,' he called, jabbing a finger at a wooden plaque on the gatepost. 'What do you think? Chocolate box, or what?'

Alix ran her eyes over the slim, thatched building, with blue-painted window-frames and a matching door. Two small mullion bedroom windows were set into the eaves. 'I think it'll do as a base. I probably could have found something better,' she replied, straight-faced.

Hamlet sighed, shaking his head.

Alix burst out laughing. 'It's beautiful, Hamlet. Come on, let's get our things and get in. I can't wait to see what it's like inside. I've always wanted to stay in a thatched cottage.'

Hamlet nodded in agreement. 'We'll get settled in, and later on I'll message Erin Scott to tell her we've arrived so we can fix up a meeting.' Hamlet gazed back towards the steep path that led the way up to Bolt Tail. 'I can't wait to hear what she has to say.'

Wave Cottage was everything they imagined a thatched cottage should be. Downstairs, a cosy lounge, with a log-burner set into an inglenook fireplace, led through to a bijou kitchen with an Aga range and stone-flagged floor. Upstairs, two good sized bedrooms gave them a sweeping view of the cove. Outside was a flagged patio on which sat a small round table with chairs. As Hamlet dumped his suitcase on his bed and threw open the small window to get a good look at the landscape, he shouted to Alix, 'This is just perfect, isn't it?'

'You've certainly delivered the goods, Hamlet!' she shouted back.

After unpacking, Hamlet took a shower, fed and watered Lucky, and then unpacked their shopping, pouring himself and Alix a glass of white wine from one of the bottles they had selected during their earlier shop. Dinner was fillet steak and a handful of new potatoes, together with broccoli florets. Hamlet had also bought a microwave Diane sauce from the supermarket in Kingsbridge. Refilling their glasses, he put the wine in the fridge and handed Alix her glass. 'Shall we sit outside and make the most of the sunshine before we eat?'

The tide was starting to come in and the few people that were down on the beach were beginning to make their way back to the harbour. Hamlet watched one couple with two young children chase their siblings along the surf's edge until they went out of view. He drank the remainder of his wine and let out a satisfied sigh. It was so peaceful here. It had been a long time since he had felt so relaxed. Even Lucky, gently snoozing by his feet, was taking advantage of the tranquillity.

Alix looked at her empty glass and held it across to him. 'Do me the honours, my good man.'

'What did your last servant die of?' he joked, snatching her glass. 'It's a good job I need another.'

'That's why I said it. I saw your glass was empty.' She chuckled.

Hamlet had noticed that she had taken to wearing loose joggers for comfort. 'How are you feeling?' he asked.

Her face flushed. 'Much better. Thank you again for rescuing me. I feel so stupid now. You caught me at a vulnerable moment, that's all. This is just what I needed.'

'Good. I needed it too.'

'And I'm deliberately going to avoid the news while I'm here. I don't want to see another bulletin about Nate and police wrongdoing. I feel as though I'm to blame for it all, even though I know I'm not.'

'Fingers crossed, our visit down here will redress things.' Hamlet nipped back into the cottage, replenished the glasses from the bottle in the fridge and returned, handing one over to Alix. The beach was now empty. The sea had come in quite considerably. Soon, the lifeboat jetty would be covered. He glanced at his watch. 'I'll finish this and then start cooking the steak.'

By the time they had prepared their meal, the evening sun was touching the tops of the trees on Bolt Tail, the blue sky replaced by a golden hue. They ate outside, washing the steak down with a couple of glasses of Côtes du Rhône Villages that Hamlet had chosen. Hamlet slipped a couple of cut-offs from his fillet to Lucky and then pushed his empty plate into the centre of the table. The beach had now completely disappeared and the earlier Mediterranean blue, green and turquoise colours of the Channel were now tinged with the orange and yellow of the evening sky.

Sitting back, Hamlet said, 'I'm so glad we made the decision not to go chasing up Bolt Tail. The drive down has wiped me out. That meal and this wine was just the ticket. I'm going to finish the bottle off and then hit the sack.'

'I'm more than happy to finish off the bottle and watch the sun go down,' Alix replied.

'An early evening it is, then,' said Hamlet, putting down his empty glass and picking up the half bottle of red. As he finished pouring them both another drink, he saw that there was enough left in the bottle for one more glass. He could already feel a soothing fatigue creeping into his body. 'I'll just let Erin know we've arrived and see what time she wants to meet tomorrow.'

Within a minute of messaging Erin, Hamlet's phone pinged. He threw Alix a mystified look. 'She said she'll meet us in a café in Kingsbridge at two o'clock tomorrow and has sent me a link. She's also asked if we can bring our IDs and says she'll explain everything.' Holding up his mobile for Alix to see the message, he said, 'Curiouser and curiouser.'

Hamlet awoke to bright sunshine creeping through a gap in the curtains. Last night he had cracked the window open a few inches before climbing into bed, and now he could hear the relaxing sound of waves breaking on the beach. He threw back the duvet, swung out his legs, stretched out some stiffness from between his shoulders and went to the bathroom. After a lazy shower, he brushed his teeth, dressed in jeans and a T-shirt and headed downstairs.

Lucky was waiting, eyeing him expectantly the moment he opened the lounge door, tail wagging furiously. Ruffling the little dog's head, he let him out into the garden. After watching him sniff around the tall bushes in the middle and do his business, Hamlet headed back into the kitchen, where he filled the kettle and switched it on. Lining up two mugs, he made himself a tea, Alix a coffee, and took hers upstairs. Tapping gently on her door, he said, 'There's a coffee outside the door for you,' before returning downstairs.

Hamlet took his tea outside and watched Lucky, now sniffing around the bottom of the garden. The tide was going out in gentle ripples, there was hardly a cloud in the sky and it still wasn't 9 a.m. *Looks like it's going to be a gorgeous day,* he thought to himself, sweeping his eyes over the cliffs of Bolt Tail. Setting his sights on the tree-lined cliff face, he knew what he was going to do with his time before the drive to Kingsbridge to meet Erin.

Putting his mug down on the patio table, he slipped back inside the cottage and picked up the Ordnance Survey map he had bought. Returning outside, he opened it to the section featuring Hope, where he folded it into a manageable square. Aligning the map to the scene before him, he found the spot where their cottage was and began tracing a finger along the features of the cove. He saw that a decent road wound its way from Inner Hope, where they were, through the hamlet of Bolberry and on to the main road into Kingsbridge. Off to the right was the promontory of Bolt Tail, which followed the coastline for at least four miles to a place called Bolt Head. The ancient remains of the Iron Age fort were only a mile from where he was, with a designated footpath that began only a dozen yards away as a set of steps next to the lifeboat station.

Hamlet lifted his eyes from the map and focused on the steps. For a hundred metres he saw that their incline was steep and narrow, disappearing into what looked like dozens of acres of woodland that stretched as far back as Bolberry. Beyond those woods lay swathes of barren land that stretched the length of the coastline to Bolt Head. This was not going to be an easy stroll, he thought to himself as he took another look at the map, fingering the route to the ancient ruins — the same route Olivia Kimble would have taken all those years ago on the night she vanished.

He wondered if the police had combed these woods during the respective searches for the two missing girls. After all, the distance between the two locations — Bolberry and Bolt Tail — was only a couple of miles. No distance at all. Surely they had?

Looking along the road from the lifeboat station to Inner Hope, Hamlet wondered where Nate Fox's former home was. He'd check it out once they had met with Erin. Hopefully, he could persuade her to show them this afternoon. He was just rearranging the map back into its original folds when Alix appeared. She was in joggers and a T-shirt, her brown hair tussled.

'I went out like a light last night,' she said. 'Did you sleep well?'

'Certainly did. Took no rocking at all.'

'I'm going to make another brew. Then I'll get us some breakfast. Fancy doing anything after that, before we meet up with Erin?'

'Funny you should ask. I've just been looking over the map. Those steps over there lead to the top of Bolt Tail. I fancy having a mooch up there to get a feel for things. What do you think?'

'Yeah, that sounds good. It'll burn off breakfast, at least.'

# ELEVEN

After a lazy breakfast, Hamlet and Alix, with Lucky in tow, crossed over the road to the lifeboat station and began their steep climb up the steps to the wood. Both of them were blowing hard as they reached the top, and after taking a minute to catch their breath, Hamlet took the lead into the woods, Lucky close on his heels.

For the first hundred yards the track was easy to negotiate, but the further they went in the more overgrown it became, with thorn bushes and swathes of ferns forcing sweeping changes of direction. The look and thickness of growth told Hamlet that no one had ventured this way in a long while. Ten minutes later, after fighting their way through brambles along a vague path broken by gnarled tree roots, they finally emerged into bright daylight. As Hamlet's eyes adjusted, he saw they had come out into a broad undulating landscape of knee-high wild grass that swept away as far as the eye could see.

'I thought there would be a path up to the ruins,' Alix said, stopping and placing her hands on her hips as she looked around.

'There should be, according to the map. We obviously went off route in the woods.' Hamlet tried to get his bearings. From the noise of the sea, somewhere to their right, he knew they were heading in the right direction for Bolt Tail. As he drifted his gaze along the meandering treeline, looking for a path, he spotted what looked like an old caravan tucked close to the trees. 'That's not what I expected to see up here.'

Alix leaned in close to him, craning her neck, following his pointing arm. 'It does look out of place. It also looks in a bit of a state.'

'Take a look?'

'Why not?' Alix replied. 'We're not in a rush.'

Setting off, neither of them could get into a good stride. The high grasses made their pace difficult, and by the time they got close to the caravan they were both blowing heavily. Only Lucky was finding the going comfortable.

The caravan was on the poky side and looked ancient. Probably from the 1960s, Hamlet guessed as he ran his eyes over it. He could just make out that its original paintwork was cream, most of the outside now covered with green moss. 'Well, it doesn't look lived in any longer,' he commented, pointing at its open door.

High grass covered the ground all around the caravan, and they couldn't make out the base of it until they came to a halt in front. The tyre on their side was flat, listing the van slightly. They saw a set of rusting steps leading up to the open doorway, but the gloomy interior prevented them from seeing any further inside. Alix went up first, testing each step before she added her weight. Hamlet was at her shoulder as she stepped inside.

The place smelt of earth and mildew. The furnishings were in a bad state, probably because of the damp. Cushions from the U-shaped window seat had been strewn across the uneven floor. The kitchen area, which consisted of a rust-pitted tiny metal sink, three wall units and two double floor cupboards, were covered in mould, the wet-warped sides swamped with empty beer bottles and partly rusting cans, dirty crockery and food and drink boxes. The place had obviously been lived in at some point, but not for a while, considering its state.

'Nothing for us here,' said Alix, turning. 'This place looks like it's been turned over, and it certainly doesn't look to me as though anyone has been living here recently.'

Hamlet had to agree. Glancing at his watch, he said, 'I was hoping to make it to the ruins, have a look round and maybe even see if we could find Nate's old house, but we haven't got time now if we're going to grab some lunch before we meet Erin. Shall we save this journey for tomorrow, after we've talked to her?'

Alix came out of the caravan, nodding. Taking a breath of fresh air, she said, 'Yes, there's no rush. I can't wait to hear what Erin has to say.'

They arrived half an hour early in Kingsbridge and found a pay and display carpark squashed between the supermarket they had visited the previous day and the top of the High Street, where Erin Scott had said the café was. Hamlet paid for three hours' parking, and after locking the car he and Alix set off to find it.

They found it easily. The café was less than a hundred yards from the carpark, an old building with a portico, giving it character. The majority of the seating area downstairs was glass-fronted, giving customers a good view of the High Street, and as they strolled towards the entrance they glanced in to see if any of the clients were on the lookout for them. Hamlet saw that a lot of the tables were taken, though no one gave him or Alix the slightest bit of attention. Seeing that there were still ten minutes until the appointed time, they chose an empty table towards the back, ordered two lattes, and waited.

The coffees arrived quickly, and Hamlet was about to take a sip when his mobile rang. Wrestling it from his jeans pocket, he saw it was Erin's number and answered. Before he could say anything, a panicked voice came on the line. 'Detective Mottrell,' she said.

He instantly knew something was wrong. 'Erin? What's the matter? Where are you?'

'Are you and Alix at the café?' she said.

'Yes, we're waiting for you. What's the matter? You sound as if you're in trouble.'

'Oh Christ, someone's following us.'

Her voice had ratcheted up in volume. He saw a couple of nearby customers turn their heads in his direction and he cupped his phone with his hand. Dropping his voice a few notches, he said, 'What do you mean, you're being followed, Erin? Who's following you?'

'An old Land Rover is following us. We've tried to let it pass, but it won't. It's been behind us for the last three miles. I thought it was you and Alix at first, but now I know it isn't. I'm scared.'

Trying his best to sound calm, Hamlet responded, 'Listen, Erin, are you in a built-up area?'

'No. It's getting closer.'

It sounded to Hamlet as if she was crying. 'Where are you?' he asked again.

She started to say something but stopped mid-sentence. He heard a dull thump and Erin cried out, 'Oh God, it's rammed us!' Before he could say anything, there was a loud scream followed by an explosion of sound, whereupon the line went dead. Pulling the phone from his ear, he stared at it and then quickly redialled Erin's number. Her phone rang out to her voicemail and he tried again. Voicemail.

'What is it? What's happened?' Alix said, her eyes wide.

More heads had turned in their direction and, conscious of straining ears, Hamlet leaned over the table and said softly, 'I think something's just happened to Erin. I think she might have crashed. She's not answering her phone.'

'Oh God! Do you know where she was?'

He shook his head. 'She didn't tell me. She said she'd been rammed just before the line went dead. She just managed to tell me it was a Land Rover. She thought it was us, that's why she rang.'

'Jesus! We don't even know where she lives, or which road she'd be on. We have no idea where she is.' Alix took a deep breath. 'We need to call the police.'

'And tell them what? We think there's been an accident, but we don't know where? What will that sound like? We don't even know what kind of car Erin was driving.'

'At least patrols can be on the lookout for her. We can't just leave it like this. She might be injured.'

'I'll try her number again.' Hamlet dialled Erin's number once more and it rang until the call transferred to her voicemail. He put his mobile down on the table. 'Let's think logically. Erin must live near Hope Cove, because she worked at the pub. We'll drive back that way now.'

Quickly paying the bill, they jogged to the Range Rover, belted up and screeched away in the direction of Hope Cove, Alix unfurling the Ordnance Survey map as Hamlet put his foot down.

They reached the outskirts of Kingsbridge within minutes, coming to a main junction that took them onto the A381 towards Hope. Hamlet passed Alix his mobile. 'Keep trying Erin's phone,' he said, and without slowing, he swung out onto the road, narrowly missing a blue saloon. He sped away to the sound of a blaring car horn.

'Bloody hell, Hamlet! Slow down. The last thing we need is to be in an accident ourselves,' Alix shouted above the noise of the revving engine. She pointed through the windscreen to a road on the right. 'We need to take that,' she said, and gripped the edge of the seat, ready for the sharp turn. As the car straightened up, she let go of her seat and rang Erin's number. Again, it went to voicemail. She waited thirty seconds and tried again. This time, it was unexpectantly answered. It was a woman and her voice sounded hesitant.

'Hello,' she said. 'Who is this?'

'Is this Erin?'

'No. This is Erin's phone. This is PC Douglas. Is it Erin you're after?'

'Yes. My name is Alix. I'm supposed to be meeting Erin. Is she there? Has something happened?'

'I'm afraid so. I'm at the scene of a serious accident. Erin is dead. Are you a friend of hers?'

In a fit of panic, Alix hung up.


It wasn't long before they came upon the crash site. A line of traffic on the main road between Kingsbridge and the turn off for Hope Cove was the first indication that something was amiss. After crawling along in a stream of slow-moving vehicles for half a mile, they saw emergency vehicles parked nose-to-tail on the opposite side, all with their top lights flashing. There were three police vehicles, two fire engines and an ambulance and paramedic vehicle.

'Jesus,' Alix breathed as they inched their way past a damaged breach in the hedgerow lining the road. A police officer was in the process of stringing out blue and white tape across the gap while beyond him, in a wheat field, they caught sight of an upturned saloon, its roof flattened. Firefighters trained a hose on burning rows of wheat stalks surrounding the smouldering remains of the car. Hamlet powered down his window as they crept along and was instantly met by the nauseating smell of burned rubber and petrol fumes. 'Poor Erin,' he murmured as they passed the damaged hedge, losing sight of the car.

Hamlet powered the window back up as the cars in front started to pick up speed.

'What are we going to do?' said Alix. 'We know this was no accident. Erin told us she was being followed and that her car was rammed. We heard the crash. We need to tell them.'

'I hear what you're saying, Alix, but if we do that, we're going to have to explain what we're doing down here. We're already in the do-dah. We don't want to make the pile any higher.'

Alix nodded slowly. 'I feel so guilty.'

The vehicles in front were starting to pull ahead. Hamlet accelerated. 'We couldn't have known this was going to happen when we contacted her.'

'I realise that, but we can't just do nothing. We know something that could help with the investigation. It'll not just be remiss of us — it'll be a disciplinary offence if we don't pass on what we know. That police officer I spoke to has my number following my phone call. She's bound to want to speak with me again. We can't cover this up, Hamlet. We're cops. You're a cop now. We know this was no accident. Erin's been murdered, for Christ's sake.'

Hamlet gripped the steering wheel. 'Look, let's get back to the cottage and think this through. I understand the magnitude of what's happened, but I just need to process it.'

'Process it? PROCESS IT! Can you hear yourself, Hamlet? This is not a therapy session. You're a detective now, with a different set of moral obligations. I'm telling you, Hamlet, we cannot just do nothing. We know this was no accident…'

Hamlet held up a hand. 'I know, Alix,' he snapped back. 'Believe me, I get what you're saying, but let's just see if we can come up with a plausible explanation that will minimise the risk for us. It's not me I'm thinking about. It's you. It's my fault we're in this mess. That police officer who took your call is going to be tied up today with the crash. We'll see what the local news says before jumping to a decision.'

Alix let out a deep sigh. 'God, I feel awful, Hamlet. I feel sick.'

Hamlet reached across and squeezed Alix's hand. 'Me too, but we can't change what's happened. What we *can* do is decide how to make it right.'

There was an uneasy silence between Hamlet and Alix all the way back to Wave Cottage. Once there, Alix disappeared to her bedroom and Hamlet took Lucky for a long walk.

He took the top road that curled around the back of the village, bringing him down to the Hope and Anchor pub, where he stopped for a pint of beer. Although late afternoon, it was still warm, and he sat at a table outside supping his beer slowly and thinking through their situation. He finished his beer without resolving the dilemma and returned to the cottage feeling desperate and low.

On his return he prepared food for them all, but only Lucky ate well. Neither Hamlet nor Alix finished their meal. At 6.30 Hamlet turned on the TV. The accident had made the local news. Camera footage showed the line of emergency vehicles parked along the road while a female reporter announced, 'Police have confirmed a woman in her thirties has died today after her car overturned on a stretch of road near Hope Cove. Police would like to hear from anyone who may have witnessed the accident, or who saw the cream-coloured car prior to the crash.'

Alix pushed away her half-eaten plate of food and rose from the table. Without speaking she went upstairs to her room, slamming the bedroom door.

Hamlet cleared the table, washed the dishes, poured himself a glass of red wine and went outside. Lucky followed, sniffing around the garden. Hamlet sat at the patio table, sipping his wine and looking out across the bay. Half a dozen small sail boats and three small luxury cruisers were gently bobbing in the sea, and a couple of paddleboarders were making their way back to the cove.

He knew Alix was right. He had to tell the police about his phone call with Erin. The accident had to be investigated as a possible murder. Whatever the consequences, he would take them squarely on the shoulders. He was just thinking about getting another drink when his mobile rang. He set down his glass and looked at the screen. It was an unknown number.

'Hello. Dr Hamlet Mottrell,' he answered cautiously. He still hadn't got used to dropping the doctor from his title.

'Detective Mottrell?' the female voice said.

'Erin! Is that you?'

'Yes.'

'Bloody hell, Erin. We thought you were dead!'

'I almost was. My friend Natalie is dead. That Land Rover ran us off the road. I managed to get out before the car blew up.' She suppressed a sob.

'I'm so sorry to hear that, Erin. Are you okay? Where are you now?'

For a moment there was silence, and Hamlet was about to ask again when Erin said, 'I'm okay. I was lucky. Just shook up, that's all.' She paused, then said, 'I had to leave Natalie. She was dead. I couldn't do anything for her.' Erin started to cry. 'I should never have involved Natalie. It was me they were trying to silence.'

'Erin, who is trying to silence you?'

'I need to speak with you, Detective Mottrell.'

'Erin, listen, you need to go to the police straight away.'

'I can't. I don't trust the local police.'

'I can help. Where are you? I'll come and get you.'

'No. I'm safe. I'm with a friend. Don't worry. I don't want to involve the local police, but I'll talk to you. I'll contact you tomorrow.'

She ended the call.

Hamlet immediately stored the number to his phone and then ran upstairs to give Alix the news that Erin was safe.

'What does she mean about being "silenced"? And about not being able to trust the local police?' Alix asked.

Hamlet shrugged his shoulders. 'She never said. But at least she trusts us. That's the main thing. We can ask her when we meet her.'

# TWELVE

Neither Hamlet nor Alix slept well. After Erin's phone call, they had shared a bottle of wine while discussing the accident, the revelation that she was alive, and her apparent mistrust of the local police. They then spent the best part of two hours going back through Erin's blog to see if there was anything they may have missed. They found nothing. After that they waited for the local news to come on, but there was no update from the earlier broadcast and so they went to bed. The day's events made for a restless night for both of them.

The next morning the pair sat in contemplation at the kitchen table, munching through a breakfast of toast when Hamlet's pinging phone made them both jump.

'It's Erin,' Hamlet said, snatching up his mobile and scrolling quickly through her message. 'She wants to meet us in an hour at Nate's old house. She's given us the directions. It doesn't seem to be too far away.' He passed his mobile over to Alix to let her read the message. 'With a bit of luck, we should get some answers soon.'

Erin's directions took them along the narrow main road of Inner Hope, into a square where a number of pretty thatched cottages were nestled together, and then onto a steep pathway that disappeared into a dense thicket of trees. However, after a hundred yards the trees parted and they emerged into strong sunlight. To their left was a low stone wall behind which was a derelict-looking cottage, partly obscured by wild laurels.

Hamlet made his way over to a five-bar gate that stood before a wide entrance, where a path led up to the cottage. The path was overgrown and did not appear to have been trodden on in some time. 'I wonder where Erin is? She said she'd meet us here,' he said, looking at his watch.

'Well, we can have a look around while we're waiting,' Alix responded, heading for the gate. She gave it a push but it hardly moved. 'We're going to have to climb over,' she said, pointing at a rusty chain fastening it to the gate post.

Just as Hamlet was preparing to hoist himself over the wall, he spotted a hand-painted sign fastened to one of the coping stones. 'Someone's sick idea of a joke.'

'*Domus Mortis*,' Alix read out loud, looking at the sign. 'Latin is not my strong point.'

'House of Death,' Hamlet explained, pulling himself clumsily over the wall and landing with a grunt on the other side.

Alix placed two hands on top of the wall and vaulted over with ease. 'Need a little help there, Doc?' She laughed and held out a helping hand.

Hamlet brushed it aside. 'If I'd have wanted to clamber over walls for a living, I would have joined the army,' he replied brusquely, brushing the dirt from his trousers.

Alix snickered as she strolled away. 'Come on, let's have a look around this house of death, shall we?'

The front of the abandoned cottage was covered in creeping ivy. It not only clung to the walls but had found its way into the guttering and was beginning to wrap its way round the two windows built into the roofline. Downstairs, two mullion windows were placed on either side of a ramshackle porch, supposedly protecting the front door. The entire building was in a state of woeful neglect.

'This place would be worth a fortune done up,' Hamlet said, avoiding a rusted oil drum poking above knee-high grass.

Approaching the door, they saw that it was ajar and Alix stepped ahead, pushing open the weather-beaten door cautiously. It opened into the kitchen and stepping inside, they were greeted by a chill that brought with it a strong smell of damp. The room was in disarray. Chairs had been overturned and cupboard doors pulled open, revealing shelves filled with all manner of crockery and tinned goods, some of the labels peeling. Some of the tinned foods had either fallen or been thrown onto the floor, joining several old milk bottles and crushed beer cans littering the place. A table in the centre was covered with dust, and an old Bush radio and electric kettle sat in the middle, surrounded by several dirty mugs. A black Aga range, set into a brick inglenook, looked to be in remarkably good order compared to the rest of the room.

'This is so sad,' said Alix, gazing around. 'This must have been a homely place, once upon a time.'

'I agree. If this had been my place, I would have been down here as much as I could.'

Alix took a deep breath. 'Come on, let's carry on.'

Making their way across the cluttered room, they pushed open a door that led into a hallway with a staircase, the lounge door opposite. Like the kitchen, the lounge looked as if it had been ransacked. As they stepped inside, they heard several creaks above them. The noise stopped them in their tracks. Alix put a finger to her lips and pointed to the ceiling.

Two more creaks.

'Someone's upstairs,' she whispered.

Hamlet nodded.

Alix tiptoed to the bottom of the staircase. Hamlet followed, making as little noise as possible.

With one foot on the bottom stair, Alix grabbed the handrail, readying herself to launch. She shouted, 'Police! Make yourself known!'

Several more creaks followed, then a dark-haired woman wearing glasses, a pink hoody and jeans appeared at the top. She looked to be aged around thirty.

'Erin?' Hamlet and Alix said in unison.

'Yes,' she called down. 'Sorry about that. I was just checking from the window to see if you'd come alone.'

'We're alone,' Hamlet confirmed. 'I'm Detective Hamlet Mottrell. This is my colleague, Detective Sergeant Alix Rainbow. She's working with me — you can trust her. You can trust us both. How long have you been here?'

'I got here about a quarter of an hour before you arrived,' she answered, making her way down.

Alix let go of the handrail and stepped back. As Erin reached the bottom, Alix noticed that her face was grazed and had lots of little cuts. 'You look like you've had quite an ordeal. I'm so glad you're okay. You gave us quite a turn yesterday. We thought you'd been killed.' Then, 'You said on the phone that your friend died. Natalie?'

Erin's eyes filled up. 'Natalie, yes. I feel terrible that I had to leave her.'

'Do you want to tell us what happened?'

Erin gave a brief nod. 'I couldn't sleep last night thinking about it. I kept seeing Natalie's face. Bleeding. I still can't believe she's dead.' She heaved in a deep breath. 'God, it was awful. I feel terrible. It's all my fault.'

Alix gave Erin's upper arm a gentle squeeze. 'Take a deep breath, Erin. Calm yourself down. We're here now. You're safe. We'll make sure nothing happens to you. And we'll find out who ran you off the road.' Alix paused to let her words sink in. Then she said, 'To do that, we need you to go back through what happened yesterday. We need you to tell us everything you can remember.'

'I don't know if I can tell you in detail. It all happened so quickly.'

'You'll be surprised what you can remember, Erin. Trust me. Now, just take another deep breath, cast your mind back to yesterday and tell us what you can. Close your eyes before you start. That can sometimes help.'

Erin closed her eyes. 'I don't know if I can do this.'

'You can, Erin. You can. If it gets too much, just stop. Okay?'

Erin nodded. 'I'll try.'

'Good. Let's start with when you picked Natalie up. Or did she come for you?'

'I picked Natalie up,' Erin began. Her voice had lost its panic-stricken edge. She sounded calmer. 'Natalie helped me set up the blog when Livvy disappeared. She's been with me through all the trials and tribulations. If I hadn't had Natalie for support, I would have given up the blog ages ago. She wrote some of the posts. Especially when I got hassled.' Erin's chest heaved. 'That's another story. Anyway, it was Natalie who said we should speak to you. So, yesterday I picked her up, and because I was so nervous, she said she'd drive.' Her bottom lip started to quiver and she opened her eyes.

'Take another deep breath, Erin. You're doing great,' Alix said. 'So, Natalie decided to drive. You were in the front passenger seat, right?'

Erin nodded.

'And you set off to meet us at the café in Kingsbridge?'

'Yes. Natalie lives — lived — in Galmpton. The next village. We drove through Marlborough and then took the A381 to Kingsbridge.'

'How far is it to Kingsbridge from there?'

Erin thought about it for a few seconds. 'I'd say seven, eight miles. Roughly a twenty-minute run. It's a good road.'

'Okay. So, you're on the main road. What were you doing?'

'Chatting. Discussing what we were going to tell you. Debating whether to tell you everything. I'd checked you out online, Detective Mottrell, and seen your involvement in the Wedding Killer case. I was fairly sure I could trust you, but not a hundred per cent. That's why I chose a public place to meet — the café at Kingsbridge — and asked you to bring your ID.' Erin paused before continuing. 'Some of the hassle I've had involves a local detective, and I wanted to check you had no connection with the local CID.'

'We are genuine, I can assure you, Erin. And we have no links whatsoever with the local CID. We've not spoken with anyone down here yet. I would like to hear more about this detective, but right now I just want to focus on yesterday. You mentioned a Land Rover in your phone call, before the crash.'

Erin gave a sharp nod. 'Yes. Sorry. Well, as I said, Natalie and I were discussing what to tell you, and then she suddenly said, "I think we're being followed." I turned around in my seat and saw an old green Land Rover behind us. It was quite close. I said, "Are you sure?" and Natalie said that she'd noticed it when we'd turned onto the main road from Marlborough. I had another look round to see if I could see who was driving, but the sun was glaring off its windscreen and I couldn't make them out. I thought it may have been you, Detective Mottrell, and that's when I decided to phone you. After that, everything just happened so quickly.'

Erin inhaled deeply, then let the breath out slowly. 'It rammed us and I dropped my phone. Natalie was screaming. Then it rammed us again and the next thing we're smashing through the hedge and the car is rolling over and over. Then it suddenly stopped, and we were upside down. That's when I saw Natalie. Her face was covered in blood, her eyes just staring. I knew she was dead. I tried to help her. Then I saw the smoke at the front of the bonnet and I knew I had to get out. Instinct took over. I don't know how, but I undid my seatbelt and got out. I managed to roll away just before the car exploded.' She covered her face with her hands. 'I couldn't do a thing to help Natalie.' She burst out crying.

Alix embraced her. 'You're safe now, Erin. You're safe. We're here. No one can harm you now.'

For a couple of minutes Erin leaned into Alix, letting out a series of gasping sobs. Alix gently patted her back and repeated, 'That's it Erin. Just let it go.'

Soon the sobs became less violent and Erin straightened up. Wiping the tears from her cheeks, she said, 'I feel so guilty. Natalie's dead because of me. I shouldn't have let her come with me.'

'You can't blame yourself for this, Erin. This is down to whoever was driving that Land Rover,' Alix replied.

'You said the sun was glaring off the Land Rover's windscreen, but did you see anything at all of the driver? Was there more than one person in the vehicle?' Hamlet asked.

Erin shook her head. 'It all happened so fast. I couldn't see. Just an outline. It looked like they were wearing dark clothing.'

'They?' said Alix.

She shrugged. 'I think there was only one person. But I couldn't say whether they were male or female. It was just an outline. Like I say, it all happened so quickly. Natalie was just starting to speed up, trying to get away. We were panicking after it rammed us the first time.'

'Did you manage to get the number plate at all?' Hamlet asked.

'No. I never thought about that. I got on the phone and rang you. Then we were rammed. All I could think about after the crash was getting away. And that's what I did. I just ran. I didn't want to go home because whoever did this probably knows where I live. So I went to my friend Lisa's, and told her what had happened. She wanted to call the police, but I told her not to. I was too scared.'

'Is that where you were yesterday evening, when you phoned me?' asked Hamlet.

Erin nodded.

'And you still haven't told the police?' Alix interjected.

She shook her head vigorously. 'No, I daren't.'

'Why not?'

'It's a long story.'

Hamlet smiled. 'That's okay. We've got all day. And I'm a good listener.'

# THIRTEEN

They decided to talk outside. Stepping out of the chilly, damp-smelling house, they were met by warm sunshine, the blue sky devoid of any cloud.

Gazing around, Erin said, 'It's such a shame the house has got into this state. This used to be a beautiful place. The garden wasn't like it is now, overgrown and full of weeds. It was once full of colour. I remember it being full of flowers and the lawn had stripes in it. We used to joke about how immaculate it was. Joe and Kate always seemed to be in it when we came up at weekends. It changed after their deaths. It became a dark place.'

'You used to come here?' Alix asked.

Erin nodded. 'Oh yes. Regularly. Me, Natalie, Livvy and some of our other friends used to come here when we were at school with Nate. Mostly on Fridays or Saturdays, when Nate's parents had gone out. Livvy and Sasha were into music in a big way and they used to play their guitars and sing together. Nate and Ross would buy the cider. We had some great times here.'

'You've mentioned a few names there, Erin, which we'll come back to. But just now you said the house became a dark place after Joe and Kate's deaths. What did you mean?'

'The house changed because Nate changed. I suppose it was understandable, his parents dying the way they did. But he went off the rails. It happened so quickly — almost like it was a relief that he could let himself go. After Livvy disappeared, things cooled between us. We had a big bust-up over the blog. The others were against it and it caused quite a bit of friction. Then Nate went off to university in Sheffield. Natalie and I phoned him after Joe and Kate's deaths, telling him we were there if he needed us. And we went to their funeral and the inquest. That's when we sort of made up again — after the inquest. We came back here and had a few drinks. Nate said he wanted bygones to be bygones — that we'd all been friends for far too long and that Livvy wouldn't want us to fall out.

'Nate didn't go back to uni straight away. He had to sort things out with the house and the finances. That took a month or so, and then he went back. But he'd come back here most weekends and invite us all over. Wanted the company, I guess. That's when the parties started up again. Me and Natalie expected them to be low-key affairs after what had happened. But Nate just went wild. Things got wilder and wilder. It wasn't fun anymore. We felt uncomfortable, so we called it a day.'

Alix nodded. 'Who were the other friends you mentioned just now?'

'There was Ross, Nate's best friend. They were a year older. Then there was Sasha and her boyfriend Fin. He was twenty-one. Being around Sasha and Fin was great fun. They made us feel so grown up. But, as I said, within weeks of Nate's parents' deaths things changed. Nate started smoking more weed. He got it from Fin, who was always getting stoned. Don't get me wrong, we had all tried it, but it made me throw up so I didn't touch it again. Livvy was more adventurous. She fancied Ross like mad. She'd do anything to get him to notice her. She came here a few times without us, and I know that Ross had sex with her.'

Erin paused, drawing in a deep breath. Letting it out slowly, she said, 'When Livvy first disappeared, we'd all come here and talk about the police search and who they were questioning. Natalie and I had discussed creating a Facebook page and starting a blog to try and help find her. But Nate and Ross told us to leave it alone and let the police do their job. I couldn't see it being an issue, but Ross said if it got out that we had been taking drugs it could cause problems for us all. I told them that that wasn't what the blog would be about. But Ross got really angry. He told me that if I told the police then he'd kill me. Nate and Sasha calmed him down, but it caused a lot of tension and the others told me to promise I wouldn't do anything that could cause Ross problems. I promised I wouldn't, but, later on, Natalie and I talked it through and we decided to go ahead with the blog, leaving out anything to do with Ross.'

'You obviously kept your word — there is nothing about Livvy and Ross's relationship in your blog,' said Alix.

She nodded. 'Natalie and I thought Ross had been a bit of a shit, taking advantage of Livvy, but we decided not to mention it. She was only sixteen. The world didn't need to know. Anyway, it wasn't relevant to her going missing, because I knew she was okay about what had happened with him. It made no difference, though, did it? We ended up falling out the moment we started the blog.'

Hamlet shot Alix a glance. He knew that despite Erin saying that the sexual relationship wasn't relevant, it needed exploring. He said, 'You say you didn't tell anyone about what had gone on between Livvy and Ross, but did you tell the police when they started investigating her disappearance? I'm presuming you were all interviewed, being her friends?'

'Well, yes. They questioned everyone who knew Livvy. Natalie and I talked to an officer from the community team. I mentioned coming here, but I obviously left out the weed and what Livvy and Ross got up to. I told them that she fancied Ross and left it at that. We were only sixteen, after all. We didn't want to get into trouble. But afterwards Nate and Ross said I was a "grassing bitch" and that Ross had got into trouble with his dad because of me. Ross's dad came to see me, and that's when the hassle started.'

'Why did Ross's dad come and see you?' Alix asked.

'Oh, sorry. I should have told you. Ross's dad was a cop. He was a detective when Livvy disappeared. He was on the investigation.'

Hamlet shot Alix a quick look. Her eyebrows were raised. Feeling his shirt starting to stick to his back from the heat of the sun, he pointed out a metal bench over by some overgrown lilac bushes and said, 'Shall we go and sit in the shade and you can tell us about Ross, his dad, and your friends. I'd like to hear more about them.'

The shade from the bushes was instantly welcoming and they all shared the bench, Erin sitting between them.

Erin cleared her throat. 'Well, there was Nate, of course. I've known him since nursery and junior school, and we went to the local comprehensive school together. There's not really much to say about him. He was a year older than me. It's only because we both lived in Hope that we knew each other. I wouldn't say I was really close to him. He was just a friend. He was quiet, polite. The only time I saw a change in him was when he'd had a drink or a smoke.' Erin frowned. 'If you're wondering if I had an inkling that he might be the Wedding Killer, then the answer is no.' She paused to look at both of them for a moment and then continued, 'He did nothing that made me suspicious. There's nothing else I can say about him.'

Alix gave a quick nod. 'Okay. What about Ross?'

'Ross Harris. He and Nate were best mates. Now, if anyone would know if Nate had any secrets, he would be the one to speak to.'

Hamlet wrote the name down.

'He lived in the police house in Hope with his parents and younger brother, Myles. Ross's dad was the local bobby here before he became a detective. Ross and Nate went to Sheffield uni together. They both studied law. Myles was in my year. When Livvy and I started working at the pub, we'd see Nate, Myles, Ross, Sasha and Fin there most Friday and Saturday nights and we'd hang around with them after the pub shut. Nate and Ross would sneak Myles, me and Livvy the odd drink. It was Nate who introduced us to Sasha and Fin. We sort of knew Sasha from school. Sasha Byrne. She's a year older than Nate and Ross.' Erin let out a small laugh. 'They both fancied her like mad, but she hung around with the older lads at school. We only got to know her better when she started singing at the pub. She was in a band with her parents. Country music stuff. They did gigs in pubs and clubs round this part of Devon. Sasha plays the guitar and she's a really good singer. When she got older, she started gigging on her own. She's really talented and does bigger events now; she's even released her own music. She and Livvy got on well because she also played the guitar and sung a bit. They would play together at Nate's place when we went up there.

'That's how we got friendly with Harriet. When she got the job at the pub, she and Livvy hit it off straight away. Harriet told us about Glastonbury, and her dreams of one day playing there herself. Harriet also played the guitar and wrote her own songs, and was saving up to record some of them in a studio. I heard some of them. Very catchy. She'd sing them when me and Livvy went up to see her while she was camping at Bolberry.

'I have to say that we all got on well together. Harriet had a great sense of humour. She had some great stories about the

Glastonbury Festival, and she was always taking the piss out of Nate and Ross. They both tried their hardest to get her into bed. In fact, Ross spiked her drink one night at the pub, but Harriet spotted him and turned the tables by switching drinks when he wasn't watching. He got into a right state. Puked up everywhere. She told him he deserved it. Sasha and Fin were there. They thought it was hilarious. Told him he'd got what he deserved. She and Sasha became good friends after that, and Harriet would go up to Sasha and Fin's caravan and sit around the fire in the evenings, playing their guitars and singing. They even discussed forming a band together, before she disappeared.'

Hamlet's hand shot up. 'You just said that Harriet went up to Sasha and Fin's caravan. Yesterday, Alix and I came upon a derelict caravan in the woods up near Bolt Tail. Could that be the same caravan you're talking about?'

Erin nodded. 'Yes. It's been empty ever since Fin did a runner.'

'Did a runner?' Hamlet repeated.

'Yes, after Harriet and Livvy disappeared.'

'Fin disappeared after Harriet and Livvy disappeared?' said Alix, eyebrows raised.

'It wasn't like that. Fin was sort of forced to go. The police were constantly hassling him when they were investigating Livvy's disappearance. Ross's dad especially was on his back. Hated him. Fin could be a smart-ass at times and he would deliberately say things that he knew would wind the police up.'

'Like what?' asked Alix.

'Like calling the officers "Mr Plod". And whistling that tune whenever he saw one of them.' Erin began whistling. 'You know the one I mean?'

Alix smiled. 'Yeah, I've heard that before.'

'And he called Ross's dad Chief Pig.'

Hamlet and Alix froze.

'Anyway, Fin was pulled in,' Erin continued. 'Very early in the morning, when they knew he'd be worse for wear from the night before. They questioned him for hours. Ross's dad was behind it, Fin told us. Ross apologised. But Fin was cool with him. He knew it wasn't anything to do with him. They found some cannabis on him and he got busted. They charged him and he was supposed to go to court, but shortly after that that he went. Ross told us that his dad said he had gone on the run and that they were looking for him.' Erin started chuckling. 'Sorry. Couldn't help myself. It reminded me of something Fin told us. He said that he'd been growing cannabis plants not far from the caravan, which he'd been regularly cropping to sell to punters in the pub, but the police had not found them when they'd searched his van. He'd managed to destroy the plants afterwards so he couldn't get caught for growing. He made fires out of them. He joked about getting high breathing in the fumes while cooking. He said nobody had snitched on him so he was probably looking at a fine, nothing more.' Erin suddenly looked serious.

'What is it, Erin?' Hamlet asked.

'I've just thought of something Fin said. It was the Friday after they had busted him for the cannabis he had on him. Just before Christmas, it was. He was drinking alone in the pub. I was clearing up the glasses, and the landlord was trying to persuade the customers to leave. I asked him where Sasha was and he told me they'd had a row and she'd moved out of the caravan. I thought it might have been because of all the weed and drinking, but he said it was because the cops threatened to destroy her music career if she didn't grass on him. But she wouldn't. He also told me that they were trying to stitch him up over Livvy's disappearance. He'd had a good bit to drink, so I told him it was time to go home. He just tapped his nose and said, "You've no idea, have you, Erin? You're so naïve." I asked him what he meant by that and he replied, "I know something about Livvy." The landlord was nodding for me to get rid of him. Then he said, "Why don't you ask Ross how he got the blood on his shirt, the night Livvy disappeared?"

'Then he got up and left. I wanted to ask him more, but I had the glasses to clear up. I was going to ask him what he'd meant the next time I saw him. But I never got to, because he'd gone. I asked Sasha where he was, but she said she had no idea. He'd taken his things and gone. Cleared off. I've not seen him since December 2008. I'm guessing he probably went back to Ireland. I think he was from County Cork.'

'What was Fin's full name?' Alix asked.

'Fionnbharr something. I don't think he ever told us his full name. Sasha will know. And you'll be able to get his details from when he was arrested.'

'Did you tell the police what he'd said?' asked Alix.

Erin shook her head. 'No. But I got to thinking. I started wondering if Fin was hinting that Ross was somehow involved in Livvy's disappearance. And did Ross's dad know something? Was that why he was hassling Fin?' She shrugged her shoulders. 'I don't know.'

'Do you think Fin was involved in Livvy's disappearance?'

Erin shrugged. 'I'm not sure. I'd like to think not. Fin was constantly getting stoned. But, in my opinion, he was harmless.'

'What about Harriet?'

'I think Harriet had a thing for him, but as far as I'm aware it wasn't reciprocated. Sasha was all Fin had time for. He was really into her, big time. And she really liked him. Fin was also heavily into music. That's how they met. They both did a gig at some event around here and he came back here with her. He bought the caravan off a farmer at Alston, and got him to tow it up to the woods. She moved in with him and they'd write songs together. He was heavily into poetry and wrote some great ballads. Sasha recorded some of them on her CDs.'

'You wrote in one of your blog posts that Harriet mentioned that she was seeing someone local. Do you know who that person might have been? Could it have been Fin? After all, she was up at the caravan playing the guitar and writing songs.'

Erin shook her head. 'Not as far as I'm aware. I'm sure Sasha was always there when Harriet went there. I think if there was something going on between those two, Livvy would have known. And she would have told me. No, as far as I'm aware Harriet went to the caravan to sing with Sasha and Fin.'

'And what about Ross? Do you think he could have been involved in Livvy's disappearance?'

She shrugged again. 'I don't know. I've wracked my brain so much since Livvy disappeared. Natalie and I discussed all types of scenarios. Ross's name did crop up. Livvy was certainly mad on him. But why would he do anything to her? They were having sex. He'd no need to hurt her. Had he?'

'What about Nate?'

'It was no secret that Nate was jealous. He'd asked Livvy out a couple of times and she'd turned him down. He'd regularly ask if she needed any help with her homework. Livvy would secretly take the piss out of him, which he found out about from Ross. I know that made him angry and there was a bit of tension between them for a while. But he still invited her to the parties at his house, and I never saw him show any malice towards her when she was there.' She looked at Hamlet and Alex. 'But if he's been arrested for the Wedding Killer murders, he's got to be the main suspect for both Livvy and Harriet's disappearances, hasn't he?'

Hamlet and Alix glanced at each other but didn't answer, and Erin continued her story.

'Natalie and I thought that someone in our group was hiding something. Everyone was interviewed and they were all cleared of any wrongdoing. Ross's dad told me that they were all at Fin's caravan on the night Livvy disappeared, and that none of them had invited her to any party up at Bolt Tail. They had all backed each other up.' Erin paused for a few seconds and then added, 'It was after that I started getting hassled.'

'Who hassled you?' Alix asked.

'Nate and Ross, mainly. But Myles and Sasha had their tuppence worth. Nate and Ross came to the pub the weekend after they'd all been questioned, when I was working. They called me a "grassing bitch" and said that I should keep my mouth shut if I knew what was good for me. Sasha said something similar, which surprised me. She said that I didn't know what I was talking about. That was when I decided to go really heavy on the blog. I was so angry. I just knew that one of them was hiding something. Natalie was of the same opinion. That's why she helped me with the blog. And that's when the online abuse started.'

'In what respect?' asked Alix. 'Trolling?'

'Exactly,' Erin replied. 'But one of them became persistent. Telling me that I shouldn't poke my nose in where it wasn't wanted. They said that "Livvy was a tart" and that "everyone knew". Then the threats started — telling me that I shouldn't interfere if I knew what was good for me. They were from someone calling themselves "The Hope Cove Watcher". I reported them to the police.'

'Do you think it could have come from anyone in your group? Nate or Ross, for instance?'

Erin tilted her head. 'It did cross my mind when it first started. You know, in retaliation. Because they couldn't shut me up.'

'What did the police do?'

'I got another visit from Ross and Myles's dad. He wasn't very nice. He told me that he was working on Livvy's case and that they were doing all they could to find her, but that it didn't help when I pointed the finger at people when I had no evidence. He said that I should let them do their job and stop the blogs. He made it clear that his sons had been cleared. Then he came on strong, saying that I could be taken to court for libel. He accused me of interfering with a police investigation. My mum and dad thought it best to listen to him. They didn't want me to get into any trouble and risk damaging my future. So, I took a lot of the stuff down, but decided to keep the blog going for Livvy.

'I took advice from a local journalist, and she helped me to rewrite some of it. She wrote several articles for the paper that really pissed them off some more, but there was nothing they could legally do, and that's when things escalated. I got more online abuse from this Watcher person, and one day we found a rat hanging from the handle of our front door. We called the police and Ross and Myles's dad came again. He took the report and a couple of weeks later told me that they were unable to find out who was behind it. He said they'd traced the Watcher's IP address to the library at Kingsbridge, but whoever had used the computers had presented a fake library pass and they weren't covered by CCTV. He strongly advised that I took down my blog. I told him that the intimidation wasn't going to stop me, and I also told him that he should have a word with his sons about what happened to Livvy, because they were hiding something. It didn't go well at all. He was fuming. Thankfully my parents asked him to leave, but they agreed with him that I should stop doing my blog. But, as you know, I didn't. I'm a bit stubborn like that. This was for Livvy.'

'Good for you,' said Alix with a smile. 'And I'm guessing, from what you've just told us, that's why you don't trust the local police. Because of this Detective…'

'…Harris.'

'Harris,' Alix repeated. 'Do you know his first name?'

'David.'

'Is he still a detective round here?' asked Hamlet.

'He's a Chief Inspector now. I think he's still in CID. At least he was the last time I checked. He works at Salcombe.'

'And his sons — Ross and Myles. Do they still live around here?'

Erin nodded. 'Yes. Ross is a solicitor now. Has a practice in Salcombe. And Myles is a cop. In CID, like his dad.'

'That's interesting.'

'You can see now why I've got issues with the local police.'

'Do you think any of them may have been involved in running you and Natalie off the road?'

'Honestly, I don't know. I'd hate to think so. We were good friends once. It all changed with Livvy's disappearance. Then, after my last blog post, when I found out about Nate being arrested for those murders in Yorkshire, I got a threatening phone call from some bloke.'

'Any idea who?' Hamlet interrupted.

'No. I didn't recognise the voice. It sounded as if he had disguised it. It was muffled. I told him that I was going to contact the police and hung up. I blocked the number.'

'What did he say?'

'That I'd been warned once and that I should watch my back.' Despite the warm weather, Erin started to shake. 'The rat was scary, but I never thought someone would try to kill me. And now Natalie is dead because of me.' She started to cry. 'I wish this whole thing had never have happened. I should have listened and stopped the blog.'

Alix put an arm around Erin's shoulders. 'This is not your fault, Erin. But now we're here and we're going to get to the bottom of this, mark my words.'

'Could Nate be involved in any of this?'

'Not the crash, no. Nate's still locked up.'

There was a long silence, which was interrupted by Hamlet. 'Have you spoken with your parents since the accident?'

Erin nodded. 'I rang them last night from my friend's house. They were so relieved to hear I was okay. I've told them everything.'

'What about Natalie's parents? Have you told them?'

Erin's shoulders slumped. 'No. I know I should, but I don't know what to say to them. How can I tell them that Natalie is dead?'

'They're going to be worried about why she's not come home or been in touch.'

'I know. I know. But the moment whoever ran us off the road knows I'm alive, I'm in danger again.'

'But they will know soon. Someone will identify the body. Sooner or later, the police are going to want to talk to you about the crash and Natalie's death.'

'I'm scared. They've tried to kill me once. They'll try again if they know I'm alive.'

'Why not find out who the police officer is who's dealing with it and leave them a message on their voicemail, telling them that you're okay? Say that you're not injured but have been shaken up, and that you're scared that someone is trying to kill you, and leave it that for now. It'll give you some leeway. And they can inform Natalie's parents of her death.'

'I won't get into trouble?'

Alix shook her head. 'No. Hamlet's right. You will have told them you're alive. That's the main thing. It will give you some breathing space, and it'll give us some time to try and get to the bottom of this.'

Erin breathed a sigh of relief. 'Thank you.'

'Well, I think that's sorted then,' said Alix, standing up from the bench. 'You've certainly given us a lot to work on, Erin.'

'Yes,' agreed Hamlet, also rising. He paused. 'There is one more thing, before you go. Can you show me where Joe and Kate died?'

# FOURTEEN

Erin took Hamlet and Alix around the back of the house, showing them a tumbledown stone barn overshadowed by trees.

'It's in a bit of a state now,' she said, pointing out the blackened double doors to the front, two sets of broken and fire-blackened windows, and a stone-slate roof with a burned hole in its centre. 'Nate's dad used it as a workshop and garage, but after the fire Nate never bothered getting it repaired. The insurance wouldn't pay out because of Joe's suicide, even though he hadn't started the fire.'

'I think I read somewhere that the car engine overheated and caught fire while it was running,' Hamlet responded.

Erin nodded. 'Yes. That came out at the inquest.'

'Joe fitted a hose from the exhaust into the back, and that's where they found his wife, Kate, with a head injury. The inquest ruled that Joe had murdered her and then killed himself.'

'That's what the police said. We all went to the inquest to support Nate, even though we'd fallen out previously.'

'And this was in October 2008, a few months after Harriet and Livvy disappeared?'

Erin nodded. 'Yes. It was another shock. In a short space of time, Livvy disappeared. Then they found the backpack belonging to Harriet, and that kick-started another investigation — this time for Harriet. And then on top of that Joe murdered Kate and killed himself.'

'Did Nate find them — his parents, I mean?'

'Oh no. Nate was at Sheffield uni by then. He started the month before. He came back once the police told him what had happened. He stayed until after the inquest, like I said. Didn't go back until after Christmas.'

'Who found them?' Alix asked.

'One of Kate's friends. They used to go out jogging together several times a week. They'd meet down at the cove in the morning, but on that day Kate hadn't shown up so her friend came up to the house. She was surprised to find the front door unlocked and the house empty, and she started looking around. That's when she saw smoke coming from the barn and called the fire brigade. They found their bodies when they broke into the car.'

Erin pursed her lips. 'A detective at the inquest said that they had found some sleeping tablets prescribed for Kate and an empty bottle of wine and two glasses in the kitchen. They found a hammer from Joe's workshop on the kitchen floor with blood on it. The pathologist said that she had been hit twice with it, hard enough that if she hadn't died from smoke inhalation, then she would almost certainly have died from the injuries.' She took a deep breath. 'It was awful to listen to. Nate's mum and dad were such lovely people. Who would have believed Joe could do that? But then, given he was having an affair…'

Hamlet frowned, remembering one of the articles he'd read. 'Go on.'

'Yes, Joe was having an affair with a florist. That was a real surprise. I always thought that Joe and Kate were happy together. Everyone was shocked. It caused some bad feeling when it came out at the inquest.'

'How did the police find out?'

'Kate's friend, who she went jogging with, told them. Apparently Kate had suspected for several months. She had followed Joe one night and had confronted the two of them in a pub. He'd promised to end it, but she later found some text messages on his phone and told her friend she was going to see a solicitor about getting a divorce.'

'Who was the woman?' Alix asked.

'The florist who supplied the flowers to Joe's funeral business. She was almost twenty years younger than him. Nate was gutted when he found out. She was only a few years older than him. He used to chat with her when he visited his dad at the funeral parlour in Salcombe. I think he secretly fancied her. Sasha told me that when we had the wake here.'

Alix quickly asked, 'What's her name?'

'Rachel Lillard. But you'll not be able to talk to her. She left shortly after the inquest. Gave up her business. Left her boyfriend. Left everything. As I say, feelings were running high after it all came out at the inquest. It was a real scandal.'

'Any idea where she went?'

Erin shook her head. 'No idea. I didn't know her. You can talk to her boyfriend, or her parents. They might know. I'm not surprised she left. Once it was out, that was the end of her business. The communities around here are so close-knit.'

Hamlet gave a brief nod of understanding. 'And the inquest, Erin — were there any suggestions that their deaths may not have been a straightforward case of murder-suicide?'

'No. The inquest found that Kate had been unlawfully killed and Joe died by suicide.' Erin studied Hamlet's face for a moment. 'Why, are you suspicious?'

Alix laughed. 'We're detectives, Erin. We're always suspicious.'

'Does that mean you're going to look into all of this?'

'Of course,' Hamlet and Alix replied in unison.

Hamlet and Alix walked with Erin to the bottom of the lane and said their goodbyes. Erin promised to ring the officer dealing with the crash later that evening and then ambled away, head down, towards the road that took her away from Inner Hope.

As she disappeared from view, Hamlet asked Alix, 'What do you think?'

She blew out a low whistle. 'She's given us a lot to think about. Some of what she said was dynamite.'

'I don't get why none of this information was acted upon by the police.'

'You heard what Erin said. She re-wrote some of her blog posts and kept information to herself after being warned off by her so-called friends and by that detective, David Harris.'

'Now a DCI, she told us.'

'And that makes our life all the more difficult. Because of his rank, we're not exactly going to be able to ring him up and ask him why he treated her like he did.'

'Do you think he was covering up for one of his sons?' Hamlet mused.

'I'd like to think not, because he's a cop, and a senior officer at that. But the honest answer is I'm not sure. If it had been me, I'd have been suspicious about what they said they were doing the night Olivia Kimble disappeared. But you know what they say about blood ties and all that. If Erin hadn't told us about him, he would have been the first person to approach. Now we need to think up another way of getting the answers we need.'

'Let's have some food and talk it through. It's too late to do anything today,' Hamlet replied, as they dropped onto the road that led back to their holiday home.

They prepared a meal of ham, cheese and olives with some leftover ciabatta bread, adding to the table what was left of yesterday's bottle of wine. In between mouthfuls they talked.

'What are your thoughts, boss?' said Hamlet, cutting a piece of mature cheddar from a small block.

Alix grinned. 'Is that sarcasm I detect, Hamlet?'

'Me? Sarcastic? Never.' He gave her a playful smile. 'Just showing some respect for my mentor and supervisor, that's all.' Then, with a thoughtful look, he added, 'On a serious note, I'm interested to hear what you think our approach should be. We got such a lot from Erin today, and all of it warrants following up. Given that someone has tried to kill her — and in fact succeeded in killing her friend — it makes the whole situation very challenging.'

'You're not kidding there, Hamlet. The frustrating thing is we can't follow any of it up in an official capacity. Ideally, we should be passing all this information on to David Harris, but at this moment in time we don't know if he's an ally or if he's somehow involved, so we're going to have to tread very carefully. We'll need to be as discreet as possible until we get some solid evidence.'

'Even then, it's going to be difficult.'

'It is, but I think I still have the ears of Lauren and her support, especially if we find something concrete that needs acting upon.' Alix paused and said, 'So long as we play this straight.'

Hamlet dipped his head in acknowledgement. 'So how do you want to play it?'

'Well, first let's just recap on what we've got,' Alix began, taking a sip of wine and swallowing. 'We have two teenage girls, eighteen-year-old Harriet Swann and sixteen-year-old Olivia Kimble, who went missing a couple of months apart in 2008. In the case of Harriet, she was spending her summer holidays before starting university hitching around Devon, getting by on savings and money she earned from part-time jobs. We know that she was camping on farmland a mile or so from here and got work at the Hope and Anchor pub. That's where she met Erin and Olivia. She and Olivia struck up a friendship through their love of music. She was introduced to Sasha Byrne and this Fin guy, who were also into music. They spend time together at Fin's caravan, the one we found near the woods, playing their guitars and singing, and there was some talk of forming a band together. At some point Harriet met Nate, his best friend Ross Harris and his younger brother Myles. Erin didn't mention any particular friendship or relationship between Harriet and these three — although she did tell us the disturbing tale of Ross having attempted to spike Harriet's drink.

'Because she was openly travelling around the West Country, we know that her disappearance wasn't treated as suspicious until her backpack was found during the search for Olivia in August. Except for a few follow-up articles in the local papers where Harriet lived in Exeter, we know little else about the circumstances of her disappearance.'

Alix downed the last of her wine, poured herself another glass and continued. 'With Olivia, we know a little more. Olivia told Erin that she had been invited to a party up on Bolt Tail on Friday the eighth of August, but she didn't say who had invited her, or who she was going with. And that was the last time she was seen. Witnesses saw what appeared to be the glow of a fire up on The Bolt, and the police found its remnants. With regards to alibis, Erin was told by David Harris, the detective working on the case, that Sasha, Fin, Nate and the Harris brothers Ross and Myles were all at Fin's caravan until the early hours.'

Alix took a long drink. Putting down her glass, she said, 'That alibi is at the heart of this, and I personally don't believe it. Fin told Erin to ask Ross how he got blood on his shirt the night Olivia went missing, but she never got him to elaborate on that because he did a disappearing act after being charged with possession of cannabis. That comment speaks volumes. It tells us that he knew something about Olivia's disappearance and that Ross Harris was somehow involved. That is one reason why we can't sit down and talk with DCI David Harris, and why we have to do our own digging around. We need to find Fin, at the very least.'

'The other thing I picked up on,' said Hamlet, 'and I know you picked up on it as well, because I saw your face, was what Fin called David Harris…'

'Chief Pig!'

'Exactly! The same phrase our mysterious letter writer used. It's too much of a coincidence.'

Alix nodded. 'And that's why we need to find him. Erin said he originates from Ireland — County Cork. But she couldn't remember his full name.'

'Am I right that under normal circumstances, we'd be able to get all that from the police computer because he was arrested?'

'Correct. But these are not normal circumstances. We haven't got access to a police computer. And I can't ask one of the team, because it leaves a footprint if questions are asked about why he's being checked out. So, tracking him down through the system is a no-no for the moment.'

'But there is Sasha Byrne. She and Fin were an item, according to Erin. She may know where he's likely to be, and she should be easy to find. You heard what Erin said about her popularity as a singer-songwriter. She's bound to have a social media following.'

Alix agreed with a nod. 'Erin mentioned that she went home after her falling-out with Fin. That can't be too far away, if they all went to school together. We'll phone Erin first thing tomorrow and see if she's got an exact address for Sasha, and if not we'll do a search using social media.' A smile broke out on Alix's face. 'That's our plan then, Hamlet. Tomorrow, we find Sasha and see what she can tell us.' She pushed her empty glass towards the wine bottle. 'Now, you can pour your boss the last of the wine. I've earned it.'

After their meal, Hamlet and Alix opened another bottle of wine and sat outside, watching the sun go down. When Alix went upstairs for a shower, Hamlet stayed in the garden with Lucky. It was peaceful at this time of the evening. Dusk had fallen, and he could hear the gentle lapping of the sea. In that moment, he could feel himself finally relaxing.

They had learned a lot from their chat with Erin, though it had left them with more work to do. Hamlet was frustrated that he and Alix were having to operate with such secrecy when there was so much important investigative work to be done.

He found his thoughts drifting to the recent investigation. Had he got it wrong about Nate being the Wedding Killer? After all, the police had got it wrong before, when they'd suspected Hamlet of having killed his family. Was he guilty of making the same mistake? He let out a long sigh. Hopefully tomorrow they might get some answers that would set them back on course and resolve his doubts. He gazed at the dark, rugged cliff face that reached up to the fringes of the woodland lining the headland.

Suddenly his eyes caught movement at the top of the path above the old lifeboat station, where it disappeared into the trees. There was a shape. A human shape. He took a couple of steps forward, concentrating on the shadow, trying his best to pierce the darkness and make out their face. But as he neared the boundary wall, the figure stepped back into the treeline and was gone.

Hamlet stopped dead, his eyes frozen on the spot where the mysterious figure had been. But there was nothing. They had gone.

Hamlet hung around in the garden for another quarter of an hour, scouring the treeline and cliff face, but the mysterious watcher didn't show again so he went indoors and locked up. Alix had retired to bed and so he decided not to say anything to her. He made sure Lucky was comfy and then went upstairs for a shower.

Before getting into bed, he turned off the light and parted the curtains a fraction to see if the stranger had returned. He saw nothing, so he pulled the curtains together and withdrew to his bed, letting out a yawn.

Tired as he was, Hamlet didn't drop off straight away. He couldn't forget the figure he'd seen in the treeline. Was it the person who had run Erin and Natalie off the road and caused Natalie's death? Or was it the person calling themself 'The Hope Cove Watcher', who had emailed Erin?

Whoever it was, from now on he would be on high alert.

# FIFTEEN

Hamlet was awoken from a deep sleep by something jumping on top of him. Startled, his heart going into overdrive, the lapping tongue on his unshaven face quickly told him it was Lucky. He squirmed away with a moan, the terrier following him beneath the duvet.

'Didn't you hear him barking?'

Hamlet pushed the little dog away and peeked out. Alix was standing in the doorway. She was wearing a dressing gown and holding a mug of tea.

'He shot in here the moment I opened the door.'

'Sorry, Alix, I was flat out. It took me quite a while to drop off last night.'

She came into the room and put the mug down on his bedside cabinet. 'I made you a brew. Do you want some breakfast? I've put some bacon on. We've got a busy day ahead of us, you know.' She headed back to the door.

Hamlet pushed himself up. 'Lovely. I'll be down in a sec.'

Lucky jumped off the bed and followed Alix out of the room and down the stairs. Hamlet drank his tea, shaved and showered. He dressed in a shirt and jeans — smart but comfortable — and then went down to the kitchen. On the table, another mug of tea was waiting for him, together with a bacon butty. Alix was leaning against the worksurface, cradling a coffee.

'Been up long?' Hamlet asked.

'Since half seven. Went straight off and slept solid. And while you've been playing at Mr Sleepyhead, I've found out where Sasha lives. Like you said, she's got a very active social media profile. She's got her own band, you know. Country and Western. Very popular. I listened to some of her tracks on YouTube this morning. Some good tunes and a good singer.'

'Does she still live round here, then?' Hamlet asked, taking a bite of his butty.

'Yes. Not far from here. Her parents have a farm at Galmpton. Looks like a dairy farm. There are a lot of pics of her on her social media among cows and calves. I've looked it up and it's only a ten-minute drive away.'

'So, how do you want to play it?'

'Well, we're going to have to take her by surprise. We can't afford to give her the opportunity to think about what she's going to tell us. We'll go to the farm — fingers crossed she'll be there — and we'll make out we're part of the Wedding Killer investigation team and have come down for a chat about Nate. We'll tell her we're after background information on him — his early life, that sort of stuff — and see how she responds. If she proves to be chatty and open, we can go on to the events surrounding Olivia and Harriet's disappearances and see where it takes us.'

'Sounds as though you've given it some thought.'

'Well, one of us got their bum out of bed early this morning and did some work.'

Hamlet was about to respond with his tale of last night's mystery watcher, but he decided to hold his silence. He could always bring it up if the stranger appeared again.

'Well, as you're so eager, I'll just finish my breakfast and then we'll go,' he said, taking another bite of his bacon butty.

The road from Hope Cove to Galmpton was a good one, with only a few pull-ins required before they found the lane that led to Byrne Farm. The scenery was typical Devon countryside:

undulating fields bordered by lush, high hedges and trees. To their left a field was dotted with lazing cows and as Hamlet drove, he couldn't help but think how wonderful it must be to live in these picturesque surroundings. A quarter of a mile on the lane brought them into a courtyard, with buildings on three sides. On two sides stood centuries-old stone structures, making up the main farmhouse and what looked like a series of barns and outbuildings. On the third side was a large breezeblock- and aluminium-clad building that Hamlet guessed housed the cattle in winter. A man in his mid-forties, dressed in brown overalls, appeared from one of the stone outbuildings at the top of the courtyard. He was cleaning his hands on a rag.

'Can I help you?' he asked in a thick Devon accent as Hamlet and Alix climbed out of the Range Rover.

'We're looking for Sasha Byrne,' Alix responded.

He looked them up and down for a few seconds and then jerked his head towards the large barn. 'She's in the dairy at the back, cleaning it down. Shall I get her for you?'

Alix grabbed her bag from the back seat. 'No, it's okay. If you can just point us the right way.'

The man had just raised his hand in the direction of the barn opening when a tall, slim woman with long auburn hair tied back in a ponytail appeared. She was wearing a pair of cut-off denims and a stained T-shirt.

Hamlet instantly recognised Sasha from the photos Alix had shown him from her Facebook page before they had set off. Some of those photos had clearly been professional shots from her gigs, but as he looked at her now he couldn't help but think that they didn't do her justice. He recalled Erin telling them that Nate and Ross had fancied her when they were at school, and now he could see why. She was stunning.

'I heard someone mention my name,' she said, coming towards them. 'I've just finished cleaning up from milking. You are?'

'Detectives Rainbow and Mottrell,' Alix answered back, taking a step forward to greet her.

Sasha swung her gaze towards the man in overalls. 'It's okay, Frank, I can sort this. You finish mending the tractor.'

The man turned and went back into the outbuilding.

Sasha returned her gaze to Alix and Hamlet. 'From Yorkshire?' she said, slipping her hands into her pockets.

'Does the accent give us away?' laughed Alix.

'I was told you were down here,' she returned. Her face had taken on a wary expression.

'Who told you that?'

She faltered for a second and then answered, 'Just a friend. Hope is a small place.'

Hamlet instantly thought about last night's visitor. He said, 'Word spreads quickly. We only arrived two days ago.'

She shrugged her shoulders. 'Like I said, Hope is a small place. What do you want with me?'

'We're undertaking a murder investigation in Yorkshire. You might have seen it on the news recently?' Alix paused, waiting for a reaction.

Sasha dipped her head. 'The Wedding Killer.'

'Well, a detective has been arrested for those murders. His name is Nathaniel Fox.' Alix watched Sasha closely. There was no reaction to Nate's name. 'We've since learned that he once lived here, in Hope, and we'd like to speak with some of the people who knew him, to get some background information. We've been told that you and he were friends.'

Sasha didn't immediately answer. 'That was a long time ago, when we were at school. I haven't seen him for years. I don't know how I can help you.'

'Well, as I said, it's background information we're after. What he was like, his hobbies, friends, stuff like that.'

The sudden sound of a revving diesel engine and churning gravel approaching from behind made them all turn. Speeding along the lane towards them was an old green Land Rover Defender with cream roof. Hamlet and Alix exchanged a glance. The four-by-four screeched to a halt, coming to rest fifty metres away.

Hamlet took a step forward.

At that moment the Land Rover began reversing back down the lane, swinging erratically from side to side as it picked up speed, its wheels throwing up a cloud of dust.

Looking at Sasha, Hamlet demanded, 'Who was that?'

Sasha was staring after the Land Rover, her face pale. 'I don't know,' she managed to stammer out.

'If someone is threatening you, Sasha, we can protect you.'

Sasha's chest heaved. 'I don't know what you're talking about. No one is threatening me. Now, can you go, please? I've nothing to say. I can't help you.' Pausing, she took a deep breath and added, 'I'm very busy. I've a lot to do. I'd like you to go, please.'

Alix held up her hands in surrender. 'Okay, Sasha, we'll leave.' She dipped into her bag and brought out one of her cards, which she pressed into Sasha's hand. 'My number is on here. If you change your mind about talking to us, or if you need our help, don't hesitate to call.'

Flicking her head at Hamlet, Alix indicated for them to go.

'Did you get the registration?' Hamlet asked, as they set off back down the lane.

Alix shook her head. 'No such luck. Everything happened too fast. Took me completely by surprise.'

'Me too. I couldn't even see the driver.'

'I think there was only one person — the driver — in the vehicle, but I couldn't make them out.'

'It's got to be the same Land Rover that ran Erin and Natalie off the road. Why hightail it out of there if it wasn't? It's too much of a coincidence.'

'I agree. Did you see which way it went?'

'Sorry, lost sight of it. Did you see how scared Sasha was?'

Alix slowly nodded. 'She knows something. I was hoping to learn more from her today, but that Land Rover put an end to that.'

'What do you suggest we do now?'

'We try the others. We know Ross Harris is a solicitor in Salcombe and that his brother Myles is a local detective. Let's see if there's anything posted online about them. Maybe I can make some phone calls.'

'Sounds good. And I'd like to see if I can track down Rachel Lillard, the florist who was having an affair with Joe Fox around the time Harriet and Olivia disappeared. Erin said Nate used to fancy her. It would certainly be interesting to get her thoughts on the Fox family.'

'Let's get to it,' Alix said, rubbing her hands together in anticipation.

By 11 a.m. thick clouds had rolled in and the warm temperatures they had enjoyed since their arrival had plummeted, forcing Hamlet and Alix to work indoors. While Hamlet settled onto the sofa with his laptop, Alix rang DC

Katie Turner from the MIT team. They had realised they could no longer carry on their investigation without help from someone else on the team, and Katie was someone they both trusted.

Swearing her to secrecy, Alix told Katie where she and Hamlet were, what had happened since their arrival, and what she was after in terms of information. At first Katie was hesitant, worried about the trouble she could get in for helping them, but she knew Alix and Hamlet had had nothing to do with the murders and she was keen to help clear their names. Alix thanked her and then ended the call.

Hamlet looked up from the sofa to see Alix grinning. 'What's that smug look on your face for?'

She leaned forward. 'One of the Manchester officers called in to review our investigation was on a detective course with Katie. They've become good friends. Anyway, this pal confided that they haven't yet found anything untoward with our investigation. She told Katie that, so far, they think the investigation was conducted in a thorough and proper manner and they can see nothing wrong with the judgement call to arrest Nate. The are currently studying the DVDs and computer equipment we found in the cellar.'

'That's reassuring.'

'Don't get too excited. Katie also told me that Professional Standards have been spending a lot of time with Lauren and the DCI behind closed doors.'

'Should we be worried?'

'I'm not sure. It's never a good sign when Professional Standards get involved. My guess is that they are carrying out a "cover-our-arses" operation following the Home Secretary's involvement. Katie's going to keep me posted.'

'Good old Katie.'

'I've given her the names of the people we're interested in. I've told her we're particularly interested in this Fin guy. She should be able to find his details from his detention record. I've said I'll update her on everything we learn down here so that when Manchester have finished with their review, and we're cleared of any wrongdoing, we can turn our attention to the people down here in an official capacity.'

'Good play.'

'Have you found anything?'

'Glad you asked. Yes, I have. Rachel Lillard, the florist, has a Facebook page, although it's not been updated since 2008. I did some googling and made a couple of phone calls while you were speaking with Katie. First, I spoke with Rachel's mum, Mrs Lillard. She lives in Marlborough, not far from here. She told me that she provided the money to help Rachel set up her floristry shop in Salcombe. Apparently, she and Rachel's dad knew Joe's mum and dad, who set up Fox's Funeral Parlour. That's how Rachel got the contract to supply the funeral flowers.

'Mrs Lillard told me that she'd had no idea that Rachel was having an affair with Joe, and she was absolutely mortified when it came out after Joe and Kate's deaths. She told me that Rachel and her boyfriend, a guy called Steve Dobson, split up. He asked her to move out from the house they shared and she went back to her parents' house.' Hamlet paused. 'She also told me that the investigating detective was none other than David Harris.'

Alix said, 'Why am I not surprised? These are small communities and detectives often cover a wide area.' She looked thoughtful. 'I recall Erin telling us that Rachel left Hope shortly after the inquest.'

Hamlet nodded. 'Yes, she did. But that isn't the whole story. Mrs Lillard tells me that Rachel is officially listed as a missing person.'

'What?' Alix exclaimed, half-rising from her seat.

'Apparently, on the night she disappeared, the alarm had gone off at her shop and the police had rung to tell her someone had smashed the front window. Her dad said he'd go with her because of the lateness of the hour, but Rachel said not to bother, that the police would be waiting for her and that she shouldn't be too long. She rang her mum from the shop to say she was waiting for the glazer to come out and board up the window. She rang her again a little later on to tell her it had been boarded up and she was on her way home. But she never showed up.

'When she hadn't returned by midnight, Mrs Lillard rang her daughter's mobile, but it went straight to voicemail. She then called the police. They told her that officers had waited with Rachel at the shop while the window had been boarded up, but they had then left to go to another call. The police returned to the shop, where they found her car parked outside with a flat tyre. It was empty. They conducted a search around the area, but there was no sign of Rachel. The police suggested that she might have either set off to walk home because of the flat tyre, or gone to a friend's house. They told Mrs Lillard to ring in the morning if she hadn't turned up. Mrs Lillard tried Rachel's mobile many times during the night, but each time it went straight to voicemail.

'When Rachel hadn't come home by mid-morning, Mrs Lillard and her husband drove over to the shop, where they found her car. They had rung her friends to see if she was with them, but no-one had heard from her. Her silence was totally out of character, because Rachel always rang to say she was okay.'

Alix's mouth tightened. 'She could have left because of the bad feeling going around after her affair with Joe Fox came out?'

Hamlet shook his head. 'What I'm going to tell you next makes her disappearance even more suspicious.'

Alix leaned forward in her chair. 'Go on.'

'Mrs Lillard told me that early the next morning, after a sleepless night, she got a text message from Rachel's phone. She read it out to me.' He picked up a piece of paper and read, '"Hi mum. Sorry for all the hurt I've caused. I can't face anyone at the moment. Decided to go away for a while. Don't know when I'll be back. Rachel."' He looked up.

Alix frowned. 'Sounds plausible to me.'

'I thought the same, except Mrs Lillard says that her daughter never called herself Rachel. Everyone knew her as Rache. And she always signed off her texts with three kisses. This message had none. I've also spoken with her former boyfriend, Steve Dobson. He received the same text message at the same time as Mrs Lillard. He doesn't think it was from Rachel either. He also told me that they had a joint account and that Rachel hasn't drawn a penny from it since October 2008, when she disappeared. No one has seen or heard from her since that night. Steve has been questioned, but he was with pals on a stag week in Ireland and has a cast-iron alibi.'

# SIXTEEN

'So, we've got three missing women now,' Alix said, as she and Hamlet walked along the path overlooking the harbour. They had decided to go to the Hope and Anchor pub for something to eat after spending most of the afternoon going over online newspaper reports relating to the disappearance of Rachel Lillard. They had also checked to see if there was any mention of Natalie's death. There were none as yet.

'I'd like to go back to the caravan up by the woods near Bolt Tail,' Hamlet said. 'Now we know it belonged to Fin, I want to have another root around. I know the police turned it over for drugs when they arrested Fin, and I'm guessing it was visited during the police search when Olivia went missing, but they would have been looking for drugs the first time and signs of Olivia the second. I don't think it would have been considered a crime scene at the time. I think he could be a key individual in all this. Witness or suspect.'

Alix flashed him a cheeky grin. 'You're beginning to think like a detective now.'

'More sarcasm?' he asked, meeting her eyes.

She shook her head. 'No, I'm being serious, Hamlet. You're right, we should go up there again. We know that on the night Olivia disappeared, she told Erin she was going to a party up on Bolt Tail, and we know from a witness that there was a fire of some type up there, and the police found remnants of it, though no sign of a party. And we know Erin and Natalie mentioned the party to the local community bobby, after which David Harris made a point of visiting Erin to tell her that his two sons, along with Nate, Sasha and Fin, had all been questioned about Olivia's disappearance and they had all alibied one another — they were all together at Fin's caravan that night. And that might well be the case, but we can't ignore what Fin said to Erin when he was drunk at the pub, after his falling-out with Sasha; he told her to ask Ross how he got the blood on his shirt the night Livvy disappeared. So, what you've just said about the caravan being a crime scene makes sense. I suspect that the party did begin up on Bolt Tail, but then they all went back to Fin's caravan and something went on there. Only they can tell us what that was. And the only way we can put pressure on them all to talk is if we find something that will force them to answer our questions.' She gave Hamlet a thoughtful look. 'Good call.'

'Up there for thinking,' he replied with a smile, pointing to his head.

'I'm going to text Katie and ask her to parcel up a couple of forensic suits and some Luminol spray and send it via special delivery. We'll get it tomorrow, and then we can do a proper forensic search. I'll record it on my phone, just in case we need it as evidence. It's unorthodox and it could be frowned upon, but there's nothing illegal about it.' Alix gave him a friendly nudge with her elbow. 'Well done you.'

'I'll let you get the beers in now I've done my bit.'

The Hope and Anchor pub was relatively quiet, with plenty of available tables. Hamlet ordered a local beer and Alix a glass of white wine before they took a menu over to one of the tables by a window. Having enjoyed the fish and chips from their previous visit, Hamlet chose it again while Alix opted for the chicken Caesar salad. They ate their meal with very little conversation, watching customers drift in and out and playing a game of guess the tourist with lots of laughter.

By 7.30 p.m. the place was beginning to fill up with evening diners, and by 9 p.m. the pub was lively. The waitress who cleared their table informed them that a folk band would shortly be playing in the extension overlooking the carpark. Hamlet and Alix looked at one another.

'Don't know about you, but I'm ready for an early night,' Hamlet said, leaning across the table so that Alix could hear him above the noise. His sleepless night had caught up with him.

'Yeah. I'd like to be fresh tomorrow as well. Katie's messaged me to say the stuff I asked for is on its way.'

Hamlet stood up from the table. 'I'll just nip to the loo and then we'll get off.'

'I'll do the same,' Alix replied, grabbing her bag.

Hamlet came out of the toilet and looked round for Alix. She hadn't come out of the ladies' yet. He heard a couple of guitars strike up and decided to head outside to wait for her. He had only gone a few steps when he collided with a man carrying a beer, some of which slopped across his T-shirt. He glanced down at the wet patches on the man's T-shirt and then lifted his gaze up to the man's face. He was a good six feet tall and well built. Hamlet apologised and made to side-step him, but the man moved into his path, blocking his way to the exit. He didn't look drunk. Hamlet said, 'Excuse me. I need to pass, please. I'm leaving.'

The man flicked his glass and splashed Hamlet's T-shirt with beer.

Hamlet jumped back. 'Whoa, careful.'

The man's lips formed a cruel smile. 'Why, what are you gonna do about it?'

'Hey, I don't want any trouble.'

The man pushed his glass against Hamlet's chest. 'Is that so? You need to be careful. Keep your nose out of business that doesn't concern you. If I was you, I'd make my way back to Yorkshire and stop troubling folk round here.'

Hamlet wished Alix would appear. She would be able to handle this situation a lot better than he could. The only angry men he'd ever faced were the weekend drunkards in A&E as a junior doctor, and this man was certainly no drunkard. Hamlet was just about to say he was a police officer, hoping that would douse the man's antagonism, when two women slipped into the gap between them. They were holding cocktail glasses and chatting away, completely oblivious to the situation. It was a golden opportunity and Hamlet made his move. He stepped quickly to one side and slipped out through the door just as another couple were entering. As the door closed behind him, he glanced over his shoulder. The man was nowhere to be seen. He picked up his pace, heading towards the sea wall above the beach, where he stopped and heaved a sigh of relief. Who was that guy? It was obvious from what he'd said that he knew who Hamlet was. His thoughts flashed back to the previous night. The stranger among the trees. Was he the watcher?

He needed to warn Alix. She was still inside the pub and might be the man's next target. He had just reached inside his jeans for his phone when footsteps caught his attention. Running towards him was the man, and there was someone else behind him. Another man, the same height but slimmer, with dark hair. He reminded him of someone he'd seen recently.

Hamlet pocketed his phone and balled his hands into fists, but he had no time to take a swing. The big man flew at him, karate-kid style, his right foot slamming into his ribcage. The force from the kick smashed Hamlet against the sea wall, where his legs buckled. As he collapsed, another kick to the side of his head produced a galaxy of stars behind his eyes and he hit the deck. Hamlet tried to scramble away, but there was nowhere to go and more boots rained in, striking his chest and legs. One connected with his lower back, causing such excruciating pain that he thought he was going to black out. As his vision faded, several shouts invaded his brain and at the same time the blows to his body ceased. He was conscious of legs surrounding him, voices asking him if he was all right and calls for someone to phone for an ambulance. Among all this confusion, someone lifted his head and he blinked open his eyes. Alix's face was full of concern.

'Boy, am I glad to see you,' he groaned. He could taste blood in his mouth.


Hamlet eased himself up into a sitting position on the sofa and let out a moan. His ribs hurt like hell. Alix sat beside him, dabbing a wet cloth over his cheek. It stung.

He'd learned from Alix that she'd arrived just as the two men were doing a runner. One of the pub staff had heard the rumpus and had come to his rescue, along with a couple of customers. She'd followed the group out, seen Hamlet's attackers fleeing — far too fast for her to catch them — and gone to his aid. After a quick check, she'd declined an ambulance and had brought him back to the cottage.

'I can't leave you for five minutes, can I? Fighting with the locals, I ask you.'

'That wasn't my doing.'

'I know,' she smiled. 'No offence, but you haven't got it in you.' Lifting the wet cloth, she scrutinised his face. 'You're going to have a lovely shiner in the morning, and you don't need to tell me that those ribs of yours are going to be a bit tender.' Pausing, she added, 'What on earth happened?'

Hamlet told her about the confrontation in the pub and the assault outside.

'Any idea who they were?'

'Never seen the big man before, but I think I recognised his mate. He's changed a bit from the photos I've seen on Sasha's Facebook page, but it looked like Ross Harris.'

'Ross!'

Hamlet nodded. 'He was only a teenager in those photos. But it was him. I'll have a word with Erin tomorrow and see if she's got any up-to-date photos of him. If not, we'll pay Ross a visit at his work.' He eased out his back and a sharp pain made him wince.

Alix put a hand against his chest. 'Careful.'

'I need to keep moving. If I stiffen up, it's going to hurt even more.'

'I'll get you some Ibuprofen,' Alix said, rising from the sofa.

'Before you go, I need to tell you something.' She sat back down, and Hamlet told her about the stranger who'd appeared in the treeline above the lifeboat station.

When he'd finished, Alix said, 'And you think this could be the Hope Cove Watcher Erin told us about?'

Hamlet shrugged. 'Someone was watching the cottage. And after the Land Rover incident this morning and what just happened at the pub, we need to watch our backs.'

Alix looked pensive. 'It looks as though we've stirred up a hornet's nest. We're going to have to be very careful if we don't want to get stung.'

# SEVENTEEN

The operational briefing at Salcombe police station took twenty minutes. Upon its completion, officers double-checked their comms and body cameras, donned the last of their protective gear and then headed out to the yard, where their designated vehicles were waiting. 'Operation Swamp' was underway, its objective to arrest a suspect in the disappearance of Olivia Kimble in 2008.

As they swept out of the station yard the operations manager, DS Myles Harris, checked that his team would move on his call and then took up his position at the back. Their destination lay thirty minutes away. Shortly before 8.30 a.m. the convoy of police vehicles, which included a transit van of twelve search-trained officers, a SCI forensic van and a CID car, turned off the main approach road into Hope Cove and made its way over the top of the coastal village towards the target address in Inner Hope. There were no blues and twos, or high-speed approach, just a steady cruise towards the cottage.

A hundred yards from their objective, Myles radioed the leading transit to pull over. He watched the CSI van park up and he followed, tucking tightly behind it. Everyone was ready and Myles was first out, his adrenalin surging. He quickly scoured the area. Nothing stirred. They had passed a dog walker a quarter of a mile back, but that had been the only sign of anyone so far. He gave his team the thumbs-up and watched them exit the vehicles, quietly pushing their doors to and then assembling into a thin line. They tucked themselves close to the roadside wall. Everything was going to plan.

Myles gave his shotgun passenger a questioning look. Receiving a nod of approval from the operation's Gold Commander, he called, 'STRIKE! STRIKE! STRIKE!' They moved into action, leaping the low boundary wall into the garden and heading for the front of the building, where one of the officers banged on the door and shouted, 'POLICE!' Without waiting for a response, he stepped to one side to let the cop with the Big Red Key do the business. It only took two powerful strikes and the door clattered inwards, everyone piling in. The raid team instantly separated into threes, fanning out left and right, six of them dashing up the stairs. It took less than a minute for the squad to search out the five rooms in the cottage, calls of 'CLEAR!' coming on each occasion. With the last call Myles walked into the cottage, dipping his head through the doorways of the lounge and kitchen before heading upstairs. In the first bedroom, he was met by the strike team sergeant.

The burly man was removing his protective helmet. 'They've gone,' he announced, flicking his head backwards.

Myles could see all the hallmarks of hurried leaving: the wardrobe doors open, empty hangers inside, drawers pulled out and the duvet flung back on the bed.

'The other bedroom is the same,' said the sergeant. 'The bed's still warm. It looks like we just missed them.'

With a look of disgust, Myles checked the bedroom and made his way downstairs, shouting out to the search team, 'See if they've left anything that'll give us a clue about where they've gone.' Outside, the Gold Commander was waiting.

'They've gone,' Myles said, with a note of frustration. 'And not long ago, by the looks of things.' Sighing deeply, he added, 'If you ask me, Dad, someone's tipped them off.'

'Fuck,' hissed DCI David Harris.

Hiding in the trees above the lifeboat station, Alix and Hamlet peered down at Wave Cottage, cops swarming around it like wasps. They had already seen the raid squad bust open the cottage door, and they watched now as two CSI officers climbed into white suits in preparation for a forensic search. Hamlet was particularly interested in the two CID officers who were side-by-side in the garden, watching and chatting.

'See those two CIDs?' Hamlet said in a low voice.

Alix nodded.

'See the younger of the two? The tall one?'

Alix nodded again.

'I'm pretty sure that's the guy who confronted me in the pub yesterday.'

Alix gave the man a long look. 'He's certainly the same build as one of the men I saw running away.'

Taking out her phone, she zoomed in with her camera and took some photos. 'I'll show these to Erin, see if she can confirm their identity. Do you know what I'm thinking?'

'David Harris and his son, Myles. Didn't Erin say Myles was in CID and his dad is now a DCI?'

Alix nodded. 'And if that is them, then this case just got a lot curiouser.'

Hamlet gave Alix a nudge. 'Come on, let's get out of here. Thank goodness we got that call from Katie. If it hadn't been for her, my guess is that we would be in a cell by now.'

They had slung their hurriedly packed bags into the boot of Hamlet's Range Rover within ten minutes of receiving DC Katie Turner's call. It had been Hamlet's intention to high-tail it out of Hope, but Alix had pointed out that they didn't know from which direction the raid team were coming and so they had decided to hide until the coast was clear. They had driven up to the woods to see what was happening.

Back in the Range Rover, Hamlet said, 'This stinks.'

'You're telling me.'

'I can't believe someone is trying to fit me up. Again. I'm so grateful to Katie for telling us about the memory stick they found in my log pile. At least now we know what our mysterious visitor was up to that night at my cabin. Hiding the memory stick containing exactly the same footage of the murders that were on the DVDs we found at Nate's home was a neat move to make it look like the Wedding Killer is me. What did Katie say? An anonymous caller tipped Professional Standards off about it being there?'

Alix nodded. 'She overheard Jackson discussing it with Lauren. She heard them mention the raid. Well, that explains why Professional Standards have been holding behind-doors meetings with the DCI. Someone is clearly worried about you and has planted evidence to put you in the frame and divert attention from Nate. They've certainly gone to some lengths, Hamlet.'

'They bloody well have. But I wonder who it is? It can't be Nate, because he's locked up.' Hamlet's mouth set tight.

'Well, we might be able tell who it is from the CCTV footage taken at your cabin. They were dressed in dark clothing, but we should be able to get some sort of idea from their build.'

Hamlet took a deep breath. 'Slight problem there, Alix.'

Alix's eyes narrowed. 'What do you mean?'

'My system has a seven-day storage facility. After that, it's wiped. If you remember, I thought it was someone from the press trying to get a story, so I didn't save it. It'll have been wiped now.'

'Oh,' she responded, looking disappointed. Then she perked up. 'Well, at least I can back you up. I saw that footage. I can tell them there was someone at your cabin that night who shouldn't have been there. It's enough to throw doubt on it being you that hid the memory stick in your log pile.'

Hamlet was deflated. 'On that particular night, maybe. But they could argue that I hid it there another time. I'll still be hauled over the coals. It'll be just like it was four years ago. But this time, you're going to be implicated as well.'

Alix stroked her chin, thinking hard. After a moment, she said, 'One of the first things Myles and David Harris will do when they get back to the nick is track our mobiles and log in your car reg for ANPR, so we're going to have to change our sim cards and hide your Range Rover. Then we're going to have to find a safe place to stay and keep our heads down for a couple of days. That should hopefully give us enough time to find the evidence to clear your name.'

Hamlet ended the call and switched off his mobile. Then he prised out the sim and put it away in the centre console of his car. 'That's sorted. Erin's going to help us out. I've told her everything. She's going to get us a couple of replacement sims and she says I can hide my car in her parent's garage. She knows someone who owns a couple of holiday lets, and she's going to give them a call to see if one's available. She's also sorting out a rental car for us. She's coming to meet us this afternoon. In the meantime we can look over Nate's place again, as well as Fin's caravan. We've got the forensic stuff in the boot. It's better than just waiting here twiddling our thumbs, don't you think?'

'Totally agree,' Alix replied, removing the sim from her mobile. She checked that her phone could still record and store video clips and, satisfied, tucked it into the pocket of her jeans and climbed out of the car. Rooting around in the boot, she recovered the forensic suits, Luminol spray and UV light.

'Right, Nate's place is only up the lane. I don't think Myles and his dad will guess we're still hanging around, so I suggest that we have a good look around and see if we can find anything that might provide some answers as to what's going on around here.'

Calling Lucky, Hamlet and Alix set off up the tree-lined lane to the Foxes' old home, the terrier scampering ahead. Five minutes later they arrived at the barred gate and, clambering over the stone wall into the overgrown garden, they headed towards the front porch. It was exactly as they had left it after their meeting with Erin, the front door still ajar.

They climbed into their hooded forensic suits and slipped on latex gloves and shoe covers. Alix started the video on her phone as they entered. Although they had been here before, on this occasion the two detectives had a different objective. They had switched to evidence-collecting mode the moment they'd stepped over the threshold. Dust was everywhere and there was a strong smell of damp. The small kitchen window was grey and grimy. On the windowsill were two stained mugs, a ceramic vase with long-dead flowers, and a bottle of washing-up liquid, all covered in grime. On a table in the centre of the room was a yellow bowl, containing rotted and withered fruit. Next to it lay several local newspapers. Hamlet had noted the papers before, but had not looked at them. This time he did. There were three, all dated December 2008. One of them lay open at an account of the inquest into Nate's parents' deaths. The headline read 'LOVE-TRIANGLE DISCOVERY IN MURDER-SUICIDE VERDICT OF POPULAR HOPE COUPLE'.

Alix leaned over Hamlet's shoulder to get a glimpse. 'Interesting,' she said, videoing the newssheet. She lifted her mobile and slowly swept it around the room, zooming in and out on various items, and then, happy with what she'd recorded, she handed the phone to Hamlet. 'Right, shall we see if we've got anything here? You keep it recording whilst I scan the room with the UV light.'

Alix switched on the small hand-held lamp and began casting its bright light over the dusty worksurfaces and along the detritus-covered floor, moving clockwise around the room. She was meticulous in her actions, gently sweeping the light over everything. Moving past cupboards and drawers she came to the washing machine, where she halted her beam upon a series of marks. 'Got something here,' she said, spraying the area with Luminol. 'Bring the phone closer, Hamlet. Zoom in on these splodges.'

Hamlet saw half a dozen roundish shapes, all fluorescent blue under the UV light, on the bottom section of the washing machine, just below the round glass door. They looked like droplets of watercolour paint. He steadied the phone over the shapes to capture them.

'Without swabbing them, I can't say for certain that this is blood, but I bet it is,' Alix said. She opened the washing machine door, grabbed the rim of the drum, planted her feet and gave the machine a hard tug. It slid forward a few inches, then stubbornly refused to shift any further. 'It's catching on the stone floor. Come on, give me a hand. Let's pull it out and see if there's anything beneath it.'

They both began tugging. After several strenuous pulls the machine finally moved, and they dragged it out from beneath the worksurface. They moved it to one side, the better to see the flagstone floor. Even before Alix sprayed the Luminol and shone the UV lamp, they both saw the dried brown puddle.

The looked at one another and at the same time exclaimed, 'Blood!'

The moment Alix squirted and cast the light over the stain, it turned fluorescent blue. 'Are you recording this, Hamlet?'

He was.

Alix dropped onto her knees and began studying the area, crawling into the gap where the washing machine had been. After the best part of a minute, she backed out from the space. 'There's a few more splashes at the back, but nothing as significant as this stain on the floor,' she announced, switching the focus of the beam onto the sides of the washer. She stuck her head and the lamp inside the drum of the machine.

Hamlet watched a halo of light glow around Alix's head as she scrabbled around inside the machine. Suddenly, she launched herself backwards, dropping onto her rear with a thump.

'Fuck me!' she cried, looking up at Hamlet. 'You've got to see this.' She pointed inside the machine. 'Get the phone inside there.'

Puzzled, Hamlet reached into the drum with Alix's mobile, cautiously squeezing in his head and shoulders. As the light from the video recording lit up the inside of the drum, he saw what had made Alix jump. At the bottom, against the dull metal, were two white objects. Bones. His medical knowledge told him they were finger bones. Human. He photographed as well as videoed the evidence and then retreated.

Alix stood with her hands on her hips. 'They're fingers, aren't they?' she said.

Hamlet nodded. 'Definitely human,' he replied.

'We'll recover them and bag them. If they belong to any of our missing women, we should be able to get a DNA result.'

For the next half hour they covered the remaining area of the kitchen, but there were no other forensic traces of blood. They made their way into the hallway. Like in the kitchen, flagstones made up the floor. Alix sprayed and scanned the surface, and more splashes lit up fluorescent blue. These were by a doorway that led into the lounge, and Hamlet videoed and photographed them.

They had been in the lounge before, but it had only been for a quick look around. Now, Hamlet and Alix's mindset was very different. They had found evidence of bloodshed. Something serious had happened in this cottage, and now every room was under the spotlight. Pushing the door open, they stepped into the lounge, casting their eyes over every inch of the room. Hamlet immediately began his video sweep, going from corner to corner, capturing every bit of furniture and every item littering the place. As he paused the recording, Alix said, 'Just close the curtains a moment, will you?'

As he made his way across the room, Hamlet could feel icy fingers trailing up his spine. The finding of the finger bones together with the bloodstains gave him a very bad feeling. He suddenly recalled the handmade sign on the front wall. *Domus Mortis*. House of Death. That should have given him a clue as to what lay behind these walls. Watching where he placed his feet, he approached the window. A pair of tartan curtains hanging from a wooden pole framed the window and Hamlet whipped the first one across, sending out flurry of dust motes. He started to sneeze and Alix let out a giggle. 'It's all right for you!' he cried, spitting out dust. 'I've just swallowed all manner of God knows what.'

'Oh, for goodness sake, Hamlet, get those curtains shut.'

Shaking his head, he pulled the other curtain across, casting the room into gloom.

Alix switched on her UV lamp and beginning at the doorway, she carefully moved clockwise around the room. On the wall opposite the window, where a three-seater sofa was set close to the wall, she stopped and let out a gasp. The entire wall lit up under the UV light. And it wasn't just the wall. Stains trailed up and onto the ceiling, streams of blue creeping towards the light fixture.

'Have you got all this on video?' she whispered, trying to hold the lamp steady in her shaking hand.

'I'm getting it all, Alix.'

'My God! There's blood all over the place. It's even up on the ceiling. I've never seen anything like it in my career.' She followed the pattern back down the wall. Suddenly, she stopped. 'What's this?' she exclaimed.

Hamlet followed the path of light to a spot on the wall a foot or so above the back of the sofa. What he'd thought were just scratch marks on the plaster were, he realised, actually the strands of letters crudely carved into the plasterwork. His eyes followed the letters as Alix highlighted each one in turn. As she came to the last letter, she spun her head round to look at him.

Together, they blurted out the word the letters spelled out.

'DEAD.'

# EIGHTEEN

Whilst Alix bagged the bones, Hamlet checked the quality of the video clips before making a note of each of their timings for future reference. Then they headed outside, climbed out of their forensic suits and stuffed them into a backpack Alix had brought ready for the trip up to Fin's old caravan.

'We really need to make someone aware of what we've found, Hamlet. This warrants following up by a full forensic team.'

Hamlet took a deep breath. 'I don't know how we're going to do that. We're technically on the run. I'm wanted for questioning over the discovery of the memory stick hidden in my log pile, and I'm guessing you're probably wanted for assisting an offender. Katie did a terrific job tipping us off and I'm sure she's on our side, but she can't help us now without getting into a whole heap of trouble.'

Alix was silent for a moment. Then she said, 'You're absolutely right. But what we've just found is damning. Forensics really need to be here. We need to find out whose blood is in that house and who the bones belong to.' She paused for a moment, then she added, 'I think I'm going to have to take a chance on giving myself up. But not to David Harris. Lauren is my best bet. She has always supported me. I'll tell her you and I split up and I don't know where you are. Then I'll tell her about the stranger we saw at your cabin that night. Whether she believes me or not, she knows I wouldn't cover up for you if I believed you were a killer. She knows how hard I worked to prove your innocence when we thought you'd killed your family.'

Hamlet gave an understanding nod. 'It's a real dilemma. If it wasn't for David Harris and his son, Myles, I'd willingly give myself up and hand over the evidence we've just found, but I don't trust them one bit.' He held up Alix's mobile. 'This is the only evidence we've got at the moment, plus the finger bones. Without them, we've got nothing.'

Alix agreed. 'Let's see if we can find anything at Fin's caravan. Then, when Erin comes to pick us up, we can evaluate what we should do.'

Alix placed the exhibit bag in a separate part of her backpack, pocketed her phone and the two of them, with Lucky, set off in the direction of Bolt Tail.

It was harder going than they expected. They lost and found the path on several occasions, but half an hour later they entered the woodland above the lifeboat station. There, once more, their journey proved difficult. Taking a more discreet route, they lost their bearings and had to double-back to pick up the path. On one occasion they came across a small group on the trail, but thankfully they were a good hundred yards ahead and never looked back.

An hour later they spotted the side of Fin's caravan and climbed back into their forensic suits to begin their search. Before going in, they cast their gaze around the outside just to check if there were signs of anyone being here since their last visit. Hamlet could see the long grass they had flattened beginning to spring back up, and he felt reassured about continuing. He went in first, the caravan creaking and tilting as he climbed inside. The smell of damp was stronger than last time and he guessed that was due to the drop in temperature. Inside, there appeared to be no change to its condition. It was still a mess with furniture upturned, and items cluttering the floorspace from the police search all those years ago.

Alix took out her phone and handed it to Hamlet. She said softly, 'Same as before, Hamlet. You do the recording and I'll search.'

Hamlet set the video running. Noticing the battery had dropped to 53 per cent, he crossed his fingers that it wouldn't run down before the search ended. When he pointed it towards Alix, she was already on her hands and knees, sifting through the clutter on the floor. Her pace was slow, her actions methodical. She didn't move on until she had sifted through scrupulously. The seating fitted around one side of the caravan and across the window had already been removed and proved easy to search. The same applied to a set of cupboards that housed a portable television. Those had already been emptied, the contents tossed across the floor, making Alix's task easy, but bringing a sigh of despair to her lips. Hamlet tried not to smile. He had quickly learned that patience was not one of Alix's virtues.

She had already drawn the curtains across the window, sprayed jets of Luminol and activated the UV lamp, but no bright blue bloodstains had been revealed and he could sense her frustration as she moved on to the kitchen area. She gave the sink and draining board a disgusted look as she gingerly nudged aside mouldy cups and plates. A cereal packet and a box of teabags looked as though they would disintegrate if they received anything more than a gentle touch. Beneath the sink the cupboard doors were ajar, and she pulled them fully open. Except for a bucket and a couple of cleaning products, there was nothing of value and she shut them again.

She moved across to a set of drawers, none of which were fully shut. She started with the bottom drawer, pulling it open. There was an old pair of binoculars, a small wind-up radio and torch, a utility camping knife and some rusted tools. The drawer above contained paperwork that appeared to be benefit correspondence and local authority occupier enquiries. Beneath these was a bulky A5 envelope, a metal loop showing above the open lip. 'Well, what have we in here?' Alix said, picking up the envelope and peering inside. With a gloved finger and thumb, she slowly extracted a silver Egyptian ankh.

As she fully exposed the piece, Hamlet let out a gasp. 'I've seen that before.'

'You have?'

'Yes. Do you remember the photograph of Olivia where she's dressed as a goth? The one on Erin's blog? Well, she was wearing a necklace identical to that one. She was also wearing a small crucifix.'

Alix delved back into the envelope and pulled out a long silver chain threaded through a silver cross. 'Like this, you mean?'

'We definitely need a team down here, including forensics,' Alix said, climbing out of her suit. The envelope holding the ankh and crucifix was safely sealed inside a plastic evidence packet, joining the one containing the bones in Alix's backpack. Hamlet had already checked the video to ensure he'd captured the moment when Alix had discovered the envelope and its contents. He was convinced the jewellery belonged to Olivia from the photograph he'd seen on Erin's blogpost, and Alix was of the same opinion.

Hamlet phoned Erin to ask if she would drive past Wave Cottage to see if there was still a police presence there, and then meet them at the bottom of the lane by the square. She told him she was on her way in a hire car, and that she had some new sim cards for their phones. She had also sorted a place for them to take refuge.

They stuck to the same route on their return, keeping to the woods wherever they could, and when they couldn't, they wove their way through waist-high grasses, scrubland and small coppices until they reached Nate's parents' cottage.

Alix stopped and said, 'The only way we're going to get any approval for a thorough forensic search of this place is to let Lauren know what we've found and send her the videoclips.'

Hamlet was hesitant. 'I'm not sure, Alix. The moment we go to the gaffer, you know what she's going to say. We will have to give ourselves up. And I for one don't want to have to hand myself in to the Harrises. They'll lock me up and throw away the key, if they get the opportunity.'

'Now you're being ridiculous, Hamlet. Lauren will not let that happen.'

'She might have no choice. This is a different force. She can't impose her authority here. And just think about this from a different perspective for a minute. If David and Myles Harris, with Ross, are involved in Olivia Kimble's disappearance, then we've got problems. Just think about what's happened so far, since we've been down here investigating.' He tapped his forefinger. 'One, Erin, who's been helping us, has been rammed off the road and her friend has been killed. Two,' he went on, tapping his middle finger, 'God knows what might have happened to me last night had you and some of the customers not come to my aid. If that's not enough to concern us, just think what else they may have up their sleeves. David Harris has a lot of clout down here. If he is involved, he could easily twist things around to make it look as though we're guilty of a cover-up.

'Whoever is involved is certainly going to a lot of trouble to bury what happened here. And someone is trying to fit me up as the Wedding Killer. By association, you being down here with me doesn't help our cause.'

'We're in a very precarious position, aren't we?'

'We certainly are, Alix. We're going to have to come up with a good plan if we're going to convince the team I'm innocent and get them to look at Nate's house down here and Fin's caravan. And discreetly, because it's my bet that if the Harrises get wind of what we've found, those two places will go up in smoke. Even with the evidence we've got so far, it's not going to convict anyone because it wasn't obtained legitimately — we didn't have a warrant to search those premises.'

'We need to put our thinking caps on.'

'We do, but not right now. My head's mashed. What I need right now is a drink. We've had a hell of a day, and we don't know what tomorrow's going to bring. It could be a cold cell.'

When they emerged from the lane, they saw Erin waiting for them, her rental car parked beside Hamlet's.

She got out to greet them. 'Found anything?'

'It's best you don't know, Erin,' Alix replied, slipping off her backpack and giving it a reassuring pat. 'Well, not at the moment, anyway. Hamlet and I have a few things to sort out before we involve anyone else. I promise, though, once we have, you'll be the first to know.' Pausing, she continued, 'Anyway, what's this place you've found for us?'

A smile lit up Erin's face. 'I think you're going to very pleased. It's a converted hayloft on a farm near Kingsbridge. It's lovely. Only just been renovated and not even advertised yet. You're the first guests. And the couple who own the farm are lovely as well. They're friends of my parents, but I've known them a long time. I've told them that you're friends of mine, here on a surprise visit. They'll not be asking you any probing questions. In fact, you probably won't even see them. They'll be working most of the day. It's a working farm. They'll have enough to do. Oh, and there are plenty of outbuildings where you can hide your car. And I've picked up some food for you. Enough for a few days anyway, so you won't need to go anywhere while you're sorting everything out.'

Alix grinned. 'Thank you so much for going to all this trouble. You're taking a risk, you know, helping us like this.'

Erin shrugged. 'You've helped me. And you're helping Natalie and Olivia, and maybe Harriet. Now, if you want to follow me, I know all the back roads round here. With luck, we'll get to the farm without any trouble.'

The farm was way off the main highway, its access a single-track dirt road that came to an end at the farm itself. Erin drove through the courtyard, past the farmhouse to a cluster of stone buildings a fair distance away. She pulled up next to the largest of the buildings, a barn, its double doors open, and pointed for Hamlet to drive in. He drove into a gloomy, cavernous space occupied by an old tractor and hay baler, which he parked next to. As he climbed out of the Range Rover and looked around, he knew the only way they would be discovered by the police would be if someone tipped them off. The adjoining converted holiday let — aptly named 'Hayloft' — was delightful; everything was freshly painted and untouched. Hamlet could smell the new carpets the moment he walked in.

Erin handed over the keys and emptied her boot of the food she'd bought. Then they fitted their phones with the new sim cards, exchanging numbers, before Erin said goodbye, telling them she'd call in the morning.

The Hayloft had been designed as an upside-down house, with a small galley kitchen, utility room and walk-in shower room downstairs and a large comfortable dining lounge and two double bedrooms upstairs. The views from the lounge windows stretched for miles across the rolling Devon hills.

'Wow, what a place. This is better than Wave Cottage. I could live here,' Alix said. She was admiring the view, a glass of Chardonnay in her hand, which she'd found in one of the shopping bags.

Hamlet joined her at the window, holding his own glass of wine. The evening sunlight shone through the far hillside trees, burning them Indian yellow. 'It is lovely, I have to admit.' Then, following a short pause, he added, 'I don't want to put a dampener on your moment, but this is just a reprieve. We've still got to come up with something before the inevitable happens. You know the likelihood is that we're now circulated as wanted, and the moment my car hits an ANPR camera that will be it. We need to do something with that evidence we found today. That's our get-out-of-jail-free card if we can put it in the right hands.'

Still gazing at the view outside, Alix said, 'I know, I've been thinking about nothing else. I need to back up our videos. That's the first thing I need to do. Then I'm going to get someone to post the bones and jewellery to Katie and ask her to sit on them for a while. Then I'm going to see if she's come up with anything on our man Fin. We really need to find him and see if we can get him to talk. I think Fin put the ankh and cross in that envelope not to keep as trophies, not because he killed Olivia, but as an insurance policy. To protect himself. He must have dropped it or left it behind by accident. Remember what he said to Erin about the blood on Ross's shirt? I'm convinced he knows something that will help solve all of this.'

# NINETEEN

The next morning, Hamlet and Alix were in the middle of breakfast when Erin rang. Hamlet put her on speaker.

'Morning, you two. I'm on hands-free in the car. Are you at the Hayloft?' She sounded excited.

'We've not long got up,' Hamlet answered. 'Is something up?'

'I'm just driving up to Galmpton. You'll never guess who's agreed to meet with me.'

Hamlet looked across the table to Alix. He answered, 'The only person I know at Galmpton is Sasha Byrne.'

'Sasha, yes. I'm picking her up. She says she wants to talk.'

'She wants to talk?' Hamlet's eyebrows rose.

'I phoned her last night. After what you told me about the Land Rover appearing at her farm the other day I thought I'd give her a call, seeing as we were once friends. She was surprised to hear from me. I told her what had happened, about being rammed off the road by the Land Rover. I hope you don't mind, but I told her you were investigating Livvy and Harriet's disappearances and how they might be linked to the murders up in Yorkshire. I told her that someone was trying to stop me talking. I said I'd had enough and that I was helping you. That got a reaction. She told me that she'd been warned not to say anything. She said she was scared to say anything because of what might happen to her, and that she'd been threatened many times over the years. I thought that she was going to hang up on me at that point, but instead she said it was now time to put a stop to it. That it had gone too far.'

Pausing for a few seconds, Erin said, 'She knows what happened to Livvy and she's willing to talk.'

'She is?' Alix exclaimed.

'Yes, but she says she wants protection.'

'And you're going to meet her now?' interjected Hamlet.

'Yes, I've arranged to pick Sasha up. She doesn't want to talk at the farm, so I'm to drive straight over to you once I've picked her up.'

'That's great, Erin,' Alix responded. 'But please be careful. You know the kind of people you're up against. They've tried to kill you once. If you suspect that you're being followed, pull in at the first public place you see. Petrol station, McDonald's, anywhere there's likely to be CCTV. They won't follow you if they know there's a chance they'll be seen.'

'Thank you for that advice. I think I should be okay because I'm in the hire car. They won't know it's me. I'm only a mile away from Sasha's. I'll bring her straight to you. Should be with you in about half an hour.'

Erin hung up.


Sasha climbed out of Erin's car. She was wearing a green and gold striped kaftan-style top over jeans, her auburn hair hanging loose down to her lower back. She reminded Hamlet of a catwalk model from the 1960s.

Alix did the greeting, telling her she had done the right thing and reassuring her that she had nothing to fear by coming. She added, 'Erin says you've agreed to talk to us.'

Sasha nodded. She looked anxious.

'I can see you're worried, Sasha,' Hamlet said, 'but you've no need to be. We can help you.'

She drew in a deep beath and held out a hand. It trembled. 'Look at me, I'm shaking like a leaf. I've thought of nothing else since you came to the farm. I'm terrified of what might happen.'

'Nothing's going to happen, Sasha,' Alix said. 'We're here to help you. Erin's told you why we're here, hasn't she? All we want to know is what happened to Livvy. Livvy was your friend too, right? Don't you want justice for her?'

Sasha gave a gentle nod. 'Of course. I've wanted to say something for ages, but I've been too worried about what will happen to me.'

'You mean the threats?' Alix replied.

'Not exactly. The threats were more warnings. No. I'm concerned that I'll be accused of covering things up. They told me I could go to prison. That I'm just as much involved as they are.'

*Them*, thought Hamlet. *We're looking at more than one killer.* He said, 'Look, let's go inside and get ourselves a cuppa. You tell us in your own time what you know about Livvy. We'll take it from there.'

Alix and Hamlet led Sasha and Erin up to the lounge. Hamlet had rearranged the furniture so that the sofa had its back to the window. He wanted no distractions while they were interviewing Sasha. Sasha took a seat and Erin sat down beside her, offering a friendly smile.

Hamlet took the hot drinks order. Alix wanted coffee and Erin and Sasha wanted tea. He nipped downstairs to brew them, returning ten minutes later. He placed the mugs on a glass-topped table between the sofa and armchairs. Alix's phone was in the middle of the table, propped up by a book. She had set it to record while Hamlet had been in the kitchen.

Hamlet picked up his steaming mug, rested it on the arm of his chair and opened the conversation. 'Sasha, I just want to reiterate, you are under no pressure whatsoever here. Please take your time — there's no rush. If at any time you feel you can't go on, then don't hesitate to tell us. Are you okay to continue?'

She nodded. 'Yes. I just want to get this over with. It's been praying on my mind for so long. I should have said something a long time ago, but I was afraid. It was only when I spoke to Erin yesterday and she told me that Natalie was dead that I realised things had gone too far. It's time to put a stop to this.'

Hamlet said, 'Thank you, Sasha. You've made a brave decision. It can't have been easy.'

She shook her head. 'No, it wasn't. I haven't been able to sleep since your visit to the farm the other day. I knew that at some stage it would come to this. I guess I was just putting off the inevitable.'

Hamlet gave her a reassuring smile. 'Try and relax, and in your own time go ahead and tell us what you know.'

Sasha picked up her mug and leaned back. After a few deep breaths, she began. 'Livvy was at the party up on Bolt Tail that night. Ross invited her. I think you know that they were seeing one another. Livvy had always fancied him and Ross knew that. I thought he was taking advantage of her, but I never said anything.'

'Can I just interrupt you there, Sasha? You're talking about Ross Harris? And this was back in August 2008?'

She nodded. 'Yes. The night Livvy disappeared. It was Ross's idea to go up there. We'd been up there loads of times with Livvy and Harriet.' She looked between Hamlet and Alix. 'Harriet was working at the Hope and Anchor. She was from Exeter. Anyway, Ross wanted to go up there and smoke some pot with Fin. Same went for Myles, Ross's younger brother, and Nate. I wasn't in the mood. I'd had quite a bit to drink and just wanted to crash out, but Fin kept badgering me to go and I ended up agreeing.'

'So, you, Ross and Myles Harris, your boyfriend Fin, Nate and Livvy all went up to Bolt Tail?'

'Yes, once Livvy had finished work at the pub. We stopped off at the caravan first so Fin could get some spliffs he'd rolled. Ross and Nate had bought some cans of lager and we all walked up there, to the old ruin, where we lit a fire, had a few drinks and smoked a couple of spliffs. Fin, Livvy and I played the guitar and sang some of the songs we'd written. It started off as a great night.' She broke off, her gaze drifting up to the ceiling.

Hamlet guessed she was conjuring up moments from that evening. He said, 'It sounds as though you were having fun?'

She lowered her head. 'We were. Until Livvy said something about Harriet to Nate. That's when it all kicked off.'

Alix asked, 'What did Livvy say?'

'Everyone was chilling, having a smoke and a drink, when Livvy suddenly said to Nate, "What have you done with Harriet, then?" I remember wondering what on earth she was talking about. I thought she was probably stoned. But then I saw the look on Nate's face. I asked Livvy what she was on about and she just said, "Ask Nate." Well, everyone looked at him. He said something like "She's stoned", but she said, "I don't think so, Nate."

'Until that moment, I hadn't given any thought to Harriet having left back in June. I thought she'd just decided to up and go. We knew she'd been planning on heading up to Glastonbury at some point. She was a singer-songwriter, like me, and I thought she might have had an offer of a few gigs before Glastonbury. I certainly hadn't thought anything untoward may have happened to her until Livvy mentioned it that night.

'Then Livvy said something about Nate's dad and Rachel Lillard — the florist. She said Harriet had seen them carrying on. We all knew that Rachel provided the flowers for Nate's dad's funeral business. Well, Nate was furious. I've never seen him so angry. He was shouting and swearing at Livvy. He threw an empty can at her, which missed. She just laughed and said, "Tell them, Nate. Your dad's shagging Rachel, isn't he?" He told her to "shut her fucking mouth" or he'd shut it for her. Then Livvy said, "She's young enough to be his daughter, the paedo," and he just flew at her. Punched her in the face. We had to drag him off. Livvy was crying. Nate was shouting. The night was a shipwreck.

'Livvy said she was going home. I offered to go with her, but she said she was okay. Five minutes later Ross said he was going to go and see how she was and make sure she got home okay. Then Nate said he'd go with him and apologise for hitting her and off they went. That left me and Fin and Myles. I said I'd had enough and was going back to the caravan, so I left Fin and Myles up there. I can't remember what time I got back. I just crashed out. And I don't know what time Fin got back. When I woke up the next morning, he was fast asleep beside me.

'A couple of days later I found out that Livvy was missing and the police were involved. I asked Fin if he thought it was anything to do with what happened up on Bolt Tail and he was really quiet. Fin was never like that. He always had something to say, and so I asked him if he knew anything. He said he thought Ross might be involved. I asked him what he meant, and he said that he and Myles had been heading back to the caravan when they'd bumped into Ross on his own. He'd had blood on his shirt. Myles had asked him what had happened, but Ross wouldn't say anything.'

'What did you think had happened?' Alix said.

Sasha shrugged. 'To begin with, I thought that Livvy might have just got her head down somewhere. You know, hiding the bruise on her face and keeping out of Nate's way after what she'd said about Rachel Lillard and his dad. Later, Erin told me that the police were taking her disappearance seriously. That they wanted to talk to everyone who knew her. She'd told them about Livvy going to the party at Bolt Tail and asked if I knew anything about it. I panicked. I thought about the weed we'd all been smoking. I didn't want Fin to get into trouble, so I told her I didn't know anything about it.'

Sasha turned to Erin. 'I'm so sorry, Erin. I wanted to say something, but then Nate and Ross came up to the caravan. They told us that Detective Harris was involved in the investigation and that it would ruin their chances of going to uni if he found out about the cannabis, so we were to all agree that we'd been at the caravan, just having a drink and playing the guitar. And that we hadn't seen Livvy since leaving the pub. Nate and Ross went up to Bolt Tail and tidied the area up.'

Hamlet said, 'Thank you, Sasha. This gives us a clear line of enquiry. Believe me, you've done the right thing. Livvy's parents are finally going to know what happened to their daughter. What that is, we don't yet know, but what you've told us puts Ross and Nate firmly in the frame for her disappearance.'

Sasha nodded. 'I knew something had happened to Livvy because I'd not heard from her, which was unusual. I was persuaded to cover up what had gone on that night because of the weed we'd smoked. I was really stressed about it all, so I packed my stuff and went home to my parents.'

Hamlet said, 'We would like to talk to Fin, but we've not been able to track him down. We know his name is Fionnbharr and that he comes from Ireland, but we've not been able to find him. It seems that he did a runner after he was charged with possession of cannabis. Do you know where he is, Sasha, or where he's likely to be?'

Hamlet was surprised to see Sasha burst into tears.

Alix reached across to her. 'Whatever's the matter, Sasha?'

After catching her breath, Sasha blurted, 'Fin didn't do a runner. That's the rumour Ross and Myles put about. Fin's dead. He was murdered!'

# TWENTY

Sasha needed a break and went outside for some fresh air with Erin and Alix while Hamlet made them more hot drinks. Twenty minutes later they returned to the lounge, Sasha telling them she was okay to pick up where they had left off.

'Sorry about that,' Sasha said. 'I've been holding on to that for so long.'

Hamlet answered gently, 'Please don't apologise, Sasha. You've obviously struggled with a great burden for many years.'

'They said that if I told anyone, I'd go to prison for being an accessory.'

'Do you know what happened to Fin? Do you want to tell us?'

Sasha interlocked her fingers, rested them on her lap, and after short cough she said, 'I was there when they killed him. It was at Nate's house. It was after the inquest into his parents' death. The police had questioned Nate about his dad and mum, and Fin was in a state over Livvy. It was a really stressful time. We were all drinking and smoking a lot more. Especially Fin. Fin was almost chain-smoking weed. It led to a massive bust-up between us. He told me to leave him alone, so I did. I packed up my things and moved back in with my parents. I helped out on the farm, like I used to. Fin rang me a couple of times, but I could tell he was pissed off and I ended up hanging up on him.

'I had only known Harriet for a month or so, so I knew very little about her, except the music side of her life. It wasn't until they found her backpack while searching for Livvy that I started putting two and two together and thinking maybe something had happened to her as well. I had to talk to someone about it, so I went up to see Fin. We had a good chat and that's when he told me about coming across Ross with blood on his shirt the night Livvy disappeared.

'He also told me that Ross had got drunk at his caravan and confessed that he and Nate had caught up with Livvy that night, and that she and Nate had ended up having another almighty row. Livvy had said she was going to the police about him hitting her. Nate flipped and thumped her again. Livvy fell back against a tree and smashed her head. She died.

'Ross told Fin that he and Nate had buried her in a shallow grave in the woods. Several days later Ross had gone back to see where they'd buried her, but her body was gone. She'd been dug up. Ross asked Nate about it and Nate told him that he'd hidden her body. He told him to stay quiet or they'd both go to jail.

'Ross knew he'd said too much and swore Fin to secrecy. Fin hated the police, and we'd already told a pack of lies about that night, so he kept quiet.' She paused, looking between Hamlet and Alix before continuing. 'We all met up after Joe and Kate's deaths. Nate asked us to go to the inquest with him.' She looked at Erin. 'I phoned you, if you remember, to see if you were coming along. I wanted to make up. I felt awful about having a go at you about Livvy's blog. I knew you were only trying to find out what had happened to her, but I was scared.'

Erin said, 'I know that now, but I wish you had told me before, Sasha.'

Sasha nodded. 'I wanted to, but I couldn't. I hope you realise why.'

Erin gave Sasha's wrist a comforting squeeze. 'You're telling us now.'

Hamlet jumped in. 'So, what happened to Fin?'

'We sort of all made up after the inquest. We had a wake for Nate's parents at their house. Nate came out with some bullshit about Livvy not wanting us to fall out, which I knew was only for your sake, Erin, to stop you blogging. He decided not to go back to uni for a while. He told his tutor he was feeling depressed and needed some time out until Christmas, and then he spent his time getting stoned and smashed. He kept inviting Fin over because of the weed, but Fin was stressed about it. When we were all together at the house one night, Fin said something about "needing to tell the truth". Nate and Ross threatened him — told him to keep his mouth shut or we'd all end up in prison. It wasn't a nice atmosphere at all.

'The following night, Nate phoned Fin to apologise. He invited us both up for a drink. I didn't want to go, but Fin said that maybe we should. It was a bad move. Nate, Ross and Fin got stoned. They were out of their heads. I didn't want to walk back to the caravan in the dark on my own, so I left them to it and crashed in the spare room. I don't know what time it was, but I was woken up by shouting and what sounded like furniture crashing around. I was really scared. Then everything went quiet, and I heard someone running up the stairs. The next minute Ross was banging on my door. I asked him what was up and he said, "Nate's gone mental. He's killed Fin." I was terrified. I didn't know what to think.'

'What did you do?' Hamlet asked.

'What could I do? I went downstairs. When I walked into the lounge, Fin was lying on the sofa. There was blood everywhere. Nate and Ross were on their hands and knees with a bucket of water and some bleach, cleaning the carpet. I just froze. I couldn't believe it. Ross said, "Are you going stand there or are you going to help us clean up this mess?" You couldn't make it up. There was my boyfriend dead on the sofa, and they were asking me to help them clear up their mess.'

'What happened next?' asked Hamlet.

'I think I remember asking what had happened.'

'What did they say?'

'Nate said Fin had asked for it. He was going to grass them up, so he stabbed him. Then he said that if I said anything, he'd make sure I was implicated. I couldn't believe it. It was the stuff of nightmares. I just couldn't think straight. I had to get out of there. So I went to the caravan. I stayed there for days, not talking to anyone.'

Erin's mouth had dropped open.

'And you never told anyone about it?' Hamlet asked.

Sasha shook her head. 'No. I'd already lied about where we all were the night Livvy died. I now knew what Nate was capable of. I was terrified of what he might do to me. I saw Ross a few days after Fin's death. He came to the caravan to say he was sorry and that it was Nate who'd killed him. He told me that Nate and Fin had argued in the kitchen and that Fin had taken a swing at Nate. Nate had picked up one of the kitchen knives and stabbed him. He told me a couple of Fin's fingers had come off when he'd tried to grab the blade.'

Sasha paused and Erin looked like she might be sick.

'I tried to persuade Ross to go to the police with me, but he said he couldn't. He was too heavily involved. I asked him what they'd done with Fin's body and he said he didn't know. He told me he'd gone home, but Nate rang him the following morning and told him to come to the house. When he got there, Fin's body had gone and Nate was power-washing the kitchen. He said he'd helped bleach the lounge carpet and they'd burned the sofa. He thought Nate might have buried Fin somewhere in the garden. He never asked.'

'Did you speak with Nate about this?'

'No. I've not spoken with him since. I couldn't face him then and I don't want to face him now. As far as I'm concerned, he's pure evil. I'm glad you've arrested him for those murders in Sheffield. I know he killed Fin and Livvy, and it wouldn't surprise me if he also killed Harriet.'


'Do you think Sasha will be arrested for complicity?' Hamlet asked.

It was late afternoon. He and Alix were sitting at the table in the Hayloft. Erin had taken Sasha back to her house on Alix's instructions. Alix and Hamlet had also told them to lay low while they sorted out protection for them both.

'No. Although she lied to the police about where they all were on the night Livvy was killed, she hasn't done anything illegal. If we're to believe her story, and quite frankly I do, then she's simply chosen not to say anything. That's not criminal. And given all the circumstances — the threats, the murder of her boyfriend Fin, her fear of what might happen to her if she talked — CPS will look favourably on her. Plus she'll be a significant witness at Nate's trial.'

'And what about Ross?'

'Ross will be arrested. He's up to his eyes in this. He helped bury Livvy's body, and he helped clean up Nate's house following Fin's murder. Who's to say he hasn't had some involvement in Harriet Swann or Rachel Lillard's disappearances?'

'Well, at least we know who those two finger bones we found in the washing machine belong to.'

Alix gave a nod of acknowledgement. 'Yes. They must have shot into the washing machine and were missed when Nate and Ross were cleaning the place up. They've been there all that time, probably even going round with Nate's washing and not being spotted. They will help convict him. And we now know why we thought there'd been a bloodbath in the lounge. Nate used a power-washer to try and clear up, not realising he'd simply dispersed a lot of the blood up the wall and onto the ceiling.'

'We've still got to find Livvy's body, though, Alix. It's my guess Nate will have buried her close to the cottage. Maybe even in the cottage, or the barn. They're old buildings — there'll be a cellar.'

'Yes, we need to go over there and see what we can find.'

It was coming up to 6 p.m. when Hamlet and Alix arrived at Nate's former family home. They took the back roads Erin had shown them and the journey was quiet. Throughout the drive Hamlet had repeatedly checked his mirrors to ensure they weren't being tailed, and as they dropped down into Inner Hope, he inwardly breathed a sigh of relief when he saw the road was empty of vehicles.

As they bounced along the uneven track from the square of pretty thatched houses up to the derelict cottage, it started to rain. He turned on the windscreen wipers and eased off the accelerator as the entranceway to the cottage appeared, finally pulling onto the grass verge next to the barred gate. Fortunately, they had raincoats in the boot and they put them on before climbing over the low wall and making their way across the garden. Hamlet was grateful for the torch he kept in the glovebox. He switched it on as they entered the porch. In the kitchen, he swept the torch around. He was looking for anything that might indicate the presence of a cellar. Finding nothing, they made their way across the hall, checking the stairwell and moving on to the lounge. Here they heaved the furniture back against the walls and pulled back the square of carpet to reveal wooden flooring, but there was nothing that looked like an entrance.

Heaving a grunt of disappointment, Hamlet said, 'I was certain there would be a cellar in a place as old as this.'

'Me too,' Alix responded. 'Never mind. Let's try the barn.'

At the end of the hallway there was a door leading to the outside. Although it was unlocked, it was stiff and it took a good heft to yank it open. Outside the rain had strengthened and the wind had picked up, driving it across the garden in slants.

'We're going to get slightly damp,' joked Hamlet as they made a dash to the old barn, throwing themselves against the stone wall and taking cover beneath the overhanging eaves of the roof.

Alix groaned. 'I can't believe this. It's been bloody lovely weather all week and the one time we don't need rain, it's bucketing down.'

Hamlet laughed. 'Come on, let's see if these doors are open. We never looked in here when we met with Erin.'

The double doors were around the side, facing the gateway. Keeping close to the wall they slipped around to the front, only to find the doors secured by a chain that had been threaded through two large drilled holes, one in each door. Hamlet handed Alix his torch. 'Here, shine this on the chain and I'll see if I can free it.'

The chains were tightly fastened and rusted in places, restricting movement, and it took him a few minutes of laborious twisting and tugging before he could finally pull them free from the holes. Breathing deeply from the exertion, he dropped the chains to the floor and stood for a moment, listening intently. He'd made a good amount of noise removing the chain, and the last thing he wanted was to catch the attention of a passing dog walker, or someone who might phone the police. Thankfully, there was no movement on the lane and the only sound came from the hissing rain. He poked his fingers through one of the drilled holes and yanked at the door. The ease with which it opened took him by surprise and he stumbled backwards, landing heavily in a puddle.

Alix burst out laughing.

Hamlet cursed, pulling himself up quickly and shaking muddy water from his hands. 'It's not funny,' he moaned.

'Oh, but it is,' Alix chuckled, strolling into the barn.

Hamlet followed, the seat of his trousers sticking to his bottom as he walked. He was suddenly very cold. As he watched Alix sweep the inside of the barn with his torch, the strong smell of petrol and soot caught at the back of his throat. It had been fourteen years since Joe and Kate Fox had died in their smoke-filled car, surrounded by the fire that had started in the engine, yet the smell still lingered. The space was now empty. Hamlet saw a few cupboards against the wall and some metal racking. Tools hung on hooks in the wall, but other than that it was just a large space, with a hole in the centre of the roof where it had collapsed from the fire. Here rain fell through, creating a puddle, but it wasn't a big one like he would have expected. Quite small, in fact, for the amount of rain falling. He watched the glistening water and noticed that rivulets were trailing away from it across to one corner, where a pile of tarpaulin lay with several large metal oil drums. He headed over, telling Alix to aim the torch at the corner.

She followed him, targeting the beam where Hamlet was pointing.

Hamlet wrapped his arms around one of the oil drums and rolled it aside. He did the same with two more, freeing up the tarpaulin, which he picked up by one corner and flung aside. Beneath it was a rusted metal slab. Hamlet stamped on it and a hollow clang rang out. 'There's something down here,' he said. Bending down, he slid his fingers into a gap between the flagged floor and metal plate. He attempted to heave it up, but it held fast. 'It's stuck,' he said over his shoulder. 'Can you see if there's a crowbar in one of the cupboards I can use?'

Alix left him and within thirty seconds she was back, holding a long piece of metal. 'No crowbar,' she replied, 'but I've found this that might do it.'

Hamlet took the metal, jabbed it into the gap and began to prise. At first there was no movement, but as he put more of his weight on top of the bar it suddenly shifted. The metal sheet shot up, taking him unawares, and he just managed to catch himself before falling. As he straightened, he found himself looking into a dark cavern. Alix pointed the torch at it, and the light picked out a set of worn stone steps descending into darkness.

Hamlet was about to take a step down when he heard a noise behind them. They spun around just as the barn doors were yanked open. A series of bright flashes blinded them. Then a voice said, 'My, my! What have we here? The murderer returning to the scene of his crime. I've been looking everywhere for you two. You're both under arrest.'

It was Detective Chief Inspector David Harris.

# TWENTY-ONE

Hamlet took the head off his beer. It was his second that evening in the Hope and Anchor. The first had hardly touched the sides. Alix was on her second glass of wine.

Hamlet swallowed, set down his glass and gazed across the table at Alix. 'I can't believe how good this beer tastes. We could have been languishing in a cell right now drinking dishwater if it hadn't been for the DI.'

After being handcuffed and driven down to Salcombe police station, Alix had used her right to a phone call to ring Lauren Simmerson. The DI had, understandably, been more than a little concerned.

'Yeah, I'm surprised how fast she got down here. We'll both probably get a bollocking when we get back, but that's a small price to pay. At least it's stopped DCI Harris stitching us up.'

'What do you think will happen to him?'

'His career is over. Myles's too, in all likelihood. As for Ross, well, he's already singing like a bird. At the moment he's blaming everything on Nate — claims his life would have been threatened if he hadn't helped cover up what Nate did. He has admitted to being behind the wheel of the Land Rover that rammed Erin and Natalie off the road, but he says he never intended to kill them. Nate told him to scare Erin away from talking to you.

'One thing he can't deny is being with Nate when the women in the bunker were murdered. The digital forensic technicians found the recorded footage on his phone, which he downloaded onto his laptop. And they've tracked his phone signal to the bunker location. In addition, they've also found on his laptop those notes claiming to be from the real Wedding Killer that were sent to the police and media. It appears Nate's phone call for a solicitor was to Ross. So, that's how he was able to come to Sheffield and leave them under the windscreen of the police car and also distribute them while Nate was on remand in prison. It's also my guess it was Ross that was captured on your CCTV planting the memory stick to incriminate you. Quite cunning, eh?'

Hamlet took another drink before relaxing back in his chair. He said, 'Not cunning enough. Just think, if it hadn't been for Erin's blog, we would never have discovered what Nate and Ross did down here all those years ago.'

'The forensics team had been up to Nate's house and removed four bodies from beneath the barn: three female and one male. They've got to formally identify them from DNA, but we believe they're Harriet, Olivia, Rachel and Fin.'

'What about Ross's brother, Myles? And his dad?'

'David has said nothing, but Myles has come clean. He's said it was all his dad's idea — covering everything up for the sake of Ross. Myles has also admitted to attacking you. They wanted to warn you off. And he's admitted to being the mysterious watcher. Same reason — to scare Erin. And the other night he was up in the woods.' She told Hamlet that Lauren had taken formal statements from both Erin and Sasha. Nate would be formally charged with the additional murders.

'You can bet Erin will be relieved that this is all over. I'm guessing she's going to make headline news once everything comes out. The publicity she'll get for her sleuthing will give LittleMissMarple celebrity status for years.'

'And richly deserved. Her determination to get justice for Olivia has finally paid off, though I'm guessing she'll be feeling pretty low for a while now she knows the truth.'

'At least the families will get closure,' Alix said, with a thoughtful look.

Hamlet took a deep breath. 'Do you know, all of this makes me wonder if Joe did actually kill his wife and then commit suicide. Could Nate have been responsible for his parents' deaths? After all, he did kill Rachel Lillard after finding out about her affair with his dad.'

'Great minds think alike. I've been thinking the same thing. Though I doubt whether we'll ever find out. Nate hasn't confessed to any of the murders so far. We may never know why he killed Harriet. Maybe we'll pay him a visit.' Alix raised her glass. 'For now, though, we've got more important things to think about. First thing tomorrow, you and I are back as working detectives.'

'I'll drink to that,' Hamlet replied, picking up his beer.

They chinked glasses.

# A NOTE TO THE READER

Dear Reader,

I have always been a plotter and planner, sometimes spending weeks on my storyline and characters, working out twists and putting in hooks to keep the reader enthralled before embarking on the writing, but sometimes things don't go the way they were meant to, and that was the case with this story. Many weeks into the writing, I felt that the book was not panning out the way I had intended, but I couldn't figure out why. By good fortune I went on a writers' retreat with some fellow Sapere authors. Their feedback instantly highlighted the problem and a major rewrite was necessary to get back on course. That done, I ploughed on and as I was nearing the finish line more good fortune came my way in the form of a chance meeting with my former colleague Sharon Barry. Sharon is a retired detective who has worked on many major investigations, including murder cases. As is par for the course with ex-colleagues, we began to share stories. Sharon happened to talk about a particular case she had worked on before retiring. Some of the aspects of the case were so fascinating that I could not resist giving creative licence to them so that they could fit in with the ending of my story. So, thank you *Grim Reaper* for that.

I also want to thank fellow Sapere authors Adele Jordan, Elizabeth Bailey, Ros Rendle, Charlie Garratt, C V Chauhan and Linda Stratmann for pulling me out of the mire, and Amy Durant, Matilda Richards and Natalie Linh Bolderston whose editing skills have made this a better book.

Also, I want to give due acknowledgement to Alan Leonard, who won the MAT charity auction to have his name included in this book. The fact that Alan is a celebrant in real life was more good fortune. He fitted in just perfect. Alan, I hope you like your appearance in this story.

Lastly, I thank you, the reader, and all the book bloggers and reviewers who have left such kind reviews for this series. Word of mouth is such a powerful thing and without you I would have fewer readers, so, if you have enjoyed this book, would you kindly leave a review on **Amazon** or **Goodreads**. And, if you want to contact me, or would like me to give a talk about my writing journey to one of the groups you belong to, then please feel free to get in touch through **my website**.

Thank you for reading.

Michael Fowler

**www.mjfowler.co.uk**

**Sapere Books** is an exciting new publisher of brilliant fiction and popular history.

To find out more about our latest releases and our monthly bargain books visit our website:
**saperebooks.com**

Printed in Great Britain
by Amazon

45073339R00099